The Calamitous Adventures of
RODNEY AND WAYNE, COSMIC REPAIRBOYS

Book One:
THE AGE ALTERTRON

BY MARK DUNN

The Calamitous Adventures of
RODNEY AND WAYNE, COSMIC REPAIRBOYS

Book One:
THE AGE ALTERTRON

BY MARK DUNN

MACADAM CAGE

MacAdam/Cage
155 Sansome Street, Suite 550
San Francisco, CA 94104
www.MacAdamCage.com

Library of Congress Cataloging-in-Publication Data

Dunn, Mark, 1956-
  Age Altertron / by Mark Dunn.
    p. cm. — (The calamitous adventures of Rodney and Wayne, the age altertron; bk. 1)
  Summary: In a small, mid-twentieth century town that is secretly being used as a laboratory, thirteen-year-old twins Rodney and Wayne and their physicist friend, Professor Johnson, face a series of calamities including a time experiment that sends the boys from infancy to old age in just a few days.
  ISBN 978-1-59692-345-4 (alk. paper)
  [1. Time travel—Fiction. 2. Experiments—Fiction. 3. Scientists—Fiction. 4. Twins—Fiction. 5. Brothers—Fiction.] I. Title.
  PZ7.D92167Rel 2009
  [Fic]—dc22
                        2009000977

Printed in the United States of America
Book design by Dorothy Carico Smith

This book is dedicated to
the memory of my twin brother Clay
who was a little bit of Rodney
and a whole lot of Wayne

CHAPTER ONE

In which Rodney and Wayne wake one morning to discover that something isn't quite right...again

G enerally, it was Rodney who woke first, though, on occasion, his twin brother Wayne, who had a better nose for morning bacon than Rodney, would be off and down the stairs before Rodney knew it. But most often it was the younger of the two brothers who rose first and who knew first what kind of a day it was going to be.

Now, some days were fine and exactly what Rodney and Wayne expected them to be. Aunt Mildred would have breakfast waiting and a cheery "good morning" for both of her thirteen-year-old great-nephews. Sometimes there would be more than just bacon on the table. Rodney and Wayne would sit down to oatmeal with cinnamon or cinnamon buns or cinnamon toast. Aunt Mildred was quite fond of cinnamon and would sprinkle it on whatever she could, and her great-nephews Rodney and Wayne hardly ever complained (except when she put it on the scrambled eggs, because then the eggs tasted odd).

Aunt Mildred, you see, had begun craving cinnamon several months earlier when everything that was granular and sprinkle-able in the town of Pitcherville was turned to cinnamon. This included most of the herbs and spices on Aunt Mildred's kitchen herb and spice shelf, but also all the bath powder and tooth powder in town, and even all the sand in all the town sandboxes!

After breakfast on normal days, Rodney and Wayne would take off on their bikes to school and all would go as it usually did for thirteen-year-old boys who lived in medium-sized American towns back in the year 1956. School was where you learned things from a blackboard or from a film-strip, and where you ate egg-and-olive sandwiches with your best buddies, and where you argued with those same best buddies over who was the best gunslinger on television, or whether or not a Martian ray-gun had a trigger. School was where you climbed a rope in physical education class, and gave a report on a book you had read too quickly the night before, and where you spun the globe and wondered about all the people who lived in all the countries that were painted a different color from your own. School was also where you sat and stared at the big clock that hung behind your teacher's desk and where you followed the minute hand as it crept slowly toward three-thirty—the time at which the dismissal bell rang and you were free to be the kind of thirteen-year-old boy you most wanted to be.

These were the days in which men wore brimmed hats to work and women wore hats of their own that sat flat and funny upon the head. These were the long-gone days in which the milkman brought not only milk but fresh creamy butter to your door, and the egg man brought eggs, and there were also people who came to your door to sell you brushes and vacuum cleaners or came to give you something they felt was important for you to read. These were the days in which television sets had rabbit-ear antennas that sat on the top and spindly antennas affixed to the roof, antennas that would pull three whole channels down from the sky, each channel giving you every kind of cowboy story you could ask for. And the only computer in town was the one to be found at Pitcherville College. It occupied nearly every inch of one whole room where it blinked and beeped and spat out punch cards.

Then there were the *other* mornings—the mornings when things were not right at all. Sometimes Rodney would wake, still drowsy with sleep, and wonder to himself, even before he had opened his eyes: "Will this be a normal day, or will it be one of the *other* kind?" And he only needed to open his eyes to learn the answer!

One Saturday morning in September, Rodney and Wayne woke to discover that everything in their town was the color of ripe peaches. Wayne pulled back the covers from his peach-colored bed and slapped his bare feet upon the peach-colored rug that covered the peach-colored floor of the bedroom he shared with his brother. He went to the window and looked out and could hardly tell one thing from another, because the lawn, the trees, the street upon which the boys lived—everything that he could see from his window— was the same color.

Peach.

"Hey, get a load of this!" Wayne exclaimed to Rodney, as he waved him over to the window. (Rodney could hardly see Wayne's waving arm, since it was the same color as the wall.) "It looks like

3

Mr. Lipe's car just crashed into Mr. Edwards' car, and lookit over there."

"Where?"

"Where I'm pointing. Squint your eyes a little. See Mrs. Carter and Mrs. Wyatt? They're both sitting on the sidewalk rubbing their heads. It looks like they just bumped their heads together."

The boys stood for a moment longer at the window, whistling in wonderment, before putting on their weekend clothes and going down to join their aunt in the kitchen.

"It's terrible, just terrible, boys!" said Aunt Mildred in a fretful tone. "Everything is the color of peaches—everything except for peaches themselves. For some reason they're now *blue*."

Wayne picked up one of the blue peaches from the fruit bowl on the table. "I wonder if they still taste like peaches."

"Well, there's no time to find out. You must go to Professor Johnson's house this instant and ask him how long we're going to have to endure this. It's a terrible inconvenience—worse than all the others that have befallen this unfortunate town. While you are speaking to him, ask him why we deserve this—why should we always be put to such trouble? I would take you boys by the hand and run away from this place as fast as our six legs could carry us were it not for that dastardly force field that prevents any of us from leaving."

Aunt Mildred sat down in her peach-colored chair and fanned herself with a peach-colored *Ladies' Home Journal* that was otherwise useless to her now.

Wayne went to his aunt and kissed her on the forehead. He stepped back and stood, posed just the way his favorite comic book hero, Mighty Mike, stood, with one hand upon his hip and the other raised in the air as if he were about to give a speech. Standing in this silly way, Wayne proclaimed, "Have no fear, kind lady! The evil that lives behind this...this..."

"*Peachiness*," said Rodney, trying to be helpful.

"Peachiness—it will not stand! And now, my faithful companion Rodney, let us fly to the laboratory of good Professor Johnson."

Rodney hated the role of the faithful companion to Mighty Mike. The superhero's true companion, Beaver Boy, was generally ignored by Mighty Mike except when he needed a dam built.

On their way to Professor Johnson's home laboratory, the boys were careful not to collide with any trees or mailboxes or lamp-posts. "Aunt Mildred is wrong," said Rodney. "This is not the worst thing that has ever happened to the town of Pitcherville. I can think of a dozen other calamities that were much worse than this one."

Then the boys began to list all of the strange things that had happened to Pitcherville in the last eleven months. Rodney and Wayne remembered the day that the Troubles had started; it was the same day their father disappeared. It was also the day that Professor Johnson, not knowing about Rodney and Wayne's father, had come to deliver his own sad news: his laboratory assistant Ivan and two professors at his college had vanished without a clue. The Professor was going from house to house helping the police with their search. He was also curious to know if his neighbors were having the same sort of personal trouble that he was having.

The personal trouble was this: every time the Professor opened his mouth to speak, all that came out was a series of numbers. And when the Professor looked all about him, he saw nothing but numbers in all the places where words usually appeared: through-out his daily newspaper, for example, or inside his copies of *Science*

Today magazine. All the words on the street signs and store signs had also been replaced by numbers. Even the town billboards had only numbers on them. For example, the Plash Detergent billboard didn't sell Plash Detergent anymore. It sold a product called "86-42," although it had the same picture on it as before: a happy woman holding up clothes that gleamed with cleanness.

In answer to Professor Johnson's numerical inquiry, Rodney shrugged and said, "Fifty-seven."

And this was why it took two full days for Professor Johnson to learn that Rodney and Wayne's father, Mitch McCall, had also been among those townspeople who were later to be remembered as "The Vanished." Until the Professor succeeded in completing his Alpha-Numerical Transferal Machine and activating it to correct this problem of words being turned into numbers, conversations between the boys and their new professorial friend generally went something like this:

"Five-hundred-fifty-four—four-hundred-and-nine—three—twenty-two," said Rodney in a calm but worrisome voice.

"Sixty-six-thousand-and-one," said Wayne, nodding eagerly.

"Thirty-three—six-hundred-and-seventy-two," replied Professor Johnson with a perplexed look (because he had no clue what it was that the boys had just said).

"That *Pandenumberum* was far worse than this peach thing," recalled Rodney.

Wayne nodded. "And the *Hubbubblia* was even worse that *that!* The town was so full of bubbles that you could hardly move without squeaking and feeling cleaner than a person generally cares to feel."

"Remember last spring when everybody's arms turned into flippers?" asked Rodney.

"The *Flip Out*? Boy, do I!" replied Wayne. "It took me almost an hour just to put on my pajamas! And we couldn't watch any of our favorite television programs because nobody could turn the knob that switches the set on."

"And *that* lasted a whole week!"

"Because that was before we started helping Professor Johnson. Notice that he does a much faster job fixing these problems when we can lend him a hand."

"Or a flipper," added Rodney, with a grin.

CHAPTER TWO

In which the Professor and Rodney and Wayne
work together to save the town of Pitcherville (yet again)
while losing a few friends among its canine population

When the boys reached the Professor's house they found the tall, thin man (who looked a little like Abraham Lincoln, but without the beard and the stovepipe hat) diligently at work in his laboratory in the back. The laboratory had its own door, which was almost never locked. There was a good reason for this; when the professor was busy with one of his new machines, he was hardly ever aware of the sounds around him, including knocks—even very loud ones. So, Rodney and Wayne had gotten into the habit of letting themselves in and waiting for the Professor to notice their presence with a nod and a smile and a very long description of what he had just been doing. Sometimes his explanation made perfect sense. For example, he would say, "Boys, I am putting a metal plate here so all this delicate circuitry won't be exposed." At other times what he said made no sense at all. For example: "Boys, the master diode has a flux of seven when I require at least an eight-point-two."

Rodney and Wayne and the Professor had become very good friends since the day he had come to their door eleven months earlier. With their dad now gone, the twins looked up to him as sons would look up to their father. The Professor was happy to have the boys for assistants and also to have them as his friends. The life of a college physics professor—a life spent teaching and reading and working on contraptions in his home lab that would save a town from all manner of continuing calamities—was a fairly lonely life. Rodney and Wayne made good company for the solitary professor, even when they weren't handing him a wrench or a screwdriver.

"Hello, boys," said the Professor. "Your timing could not have been better. How do you like my Peach Pigment Evanescizer? I have just this minute completed its construction."

"Well," said Rodney, looking over the machine, "it looks very much like your Lemon Pigment Evanescizer."

"An astute observation," said the Professor, wiping his dirty hands on his lab coat. "It works very much like the Evanescizer we used to remove all the lemon color from the town two months ago." The Professor took a bite from the sandwich that his housekeeper and cook Mrs. Ferrell had left for him before she went off to the grocery store. It was the Professor's favorite sandwich. In fact, it was the only kind of sandwich he would eat: sardines and Swiss cheese. Rodney and Wayne had tried it themselves once and secretly called it "Professor Johnson's 'Yuck' sandwich."

"It sounds to me," said Rodney, running his hand along the smooth aluminum housing of the machine, "that the peach color will be just as easy to remove as the lemon color was."

"One would *think* so," said the Professor, extracting a small peach-colored sardine from his sandwich to give to his fish-loving half-Persian/half-Siamese cat Gizmo. Gizmo sniffed the small fish (because it didn't look familiar to her). Then, satisfied that it was fishy in nature, she took it directly from her master's hand and gobbled it down. Then she carried her very furry body over to her sleeping pillow and began to clean the fish oil from her mouth with a spitty paw.

"But here is the thing," the Professor went on. "The color known as *lemon* is very similar to its parent color *yellow*. There is very little variation in hue at all. And what do we know about the color *yellow*?"

"That it is a primary color?" asked Rodney.

"You're exactly right. Whereas peach is a combination of several different primary and secondary colors. It's a much more complicated sort of color to dispense with. So, my frequency generator will have to be tuned to a much higher pitch. And do we know what happens when a frequency generator is tuned to a higher pitch?"

Rodney shrugged. Wayne shrugged.

"Think about it, boys. It has something to do with dogs. It has something to do with every dog in the town of Pitcherville."

"I think it must be a frequency that only dogs can hear!" said Wayne proudly.

"But more than that—"

The boys thought about this for a moment but could not arrive at the answer.

"Dogs may be the only creatures to hear the high frequency, but will they like it?" hinted the Professor.

Wayne shook his head in large part because Professor Johnson was shaking *his* head to steer him to the correct answer.

"No siree, boys, they won't take to it at all. We'll have quite a bit of yelping and yowling to deal with until all the pigment has been shaken loose from this town, and you can bet that Officer Wall from the Pitcherville Police Department's Loud Noises Unit will be at my door lickety split to write me a summons. Just you wait."

"And there's no other way to do what we have to do?" asked Rodney.

"I'm afraid there isn't. It is the price that we must pay for science. Now, I have a very important job for the both of you. Here is a screwdriver for you, Rodney, and here is one for you, Wayne, and here are some canine earmuffs I have made for my little terrier Tesla. You will be custodian of those, Wayne. Now…when Tesla comes running in here howling and yowling you must catch him and put these on his ears, for it will be loudest here inside my house and I do not wish for him to be made too uncomfortable."

Wayne nodded. He held a screwdriver in one hand and the canine earmuffs in the other. "But Professor," said Wayne, "what are the screwdrivers for?"

"Perhaps your brother Rodney knows?"

Rodney thought for a moment while scratching his forehead with the business end of his screwdriver. Then his face brightened. "Well, I remember that the other machine—the one you built this one from…"

"The Lemon Pigment Evanescizer. Yes, go on…"

"Well, I remember that once it started really going, it began to rattle, and before we finished, it was rattling quite a lot, and some of the screws that were holding it together almost shook themselves out of their grooves. I suppose, Professor, that this one rattles even more than that one did."

"Your supposition is correct."

"So we'll have to work even harder to keep *these* screws from coming out."

"And to keep the Evanescizer from totally dismantling itself! Rodney, my boy, that was a crackerjack observation—quite astute, right on the money!"

Wayne's heart sank. He had been excited and eager to do his part to save the town of Pitcherville from its latest disaster, but now the happy feeling was gone. He bowed his head and looked down at the floor so that Rodney and the Professor couldn't see in his face how badly he felt.

Wayne could not help it that he felt things stronger than his brother. That was just the way he was. And it wasn't that he minded hearing that Rodney had just made a crackerjack observation that was astute and right on the money. He only wished that every now and then the Professor might say the same thing about *him.*

Wayne wondered sometimes if the Professor and his Aunt Mildred and all his friends and perhaps even his father thought he wasn't as smart as his twin brother Rodney. Once he had even found the courage to ask his Aunt about it—to find out if it were true. "Rodney smarter than you? Oh, for Heaven's sake, what a question!" she had replied. As she tousled his hair with affection, she had added, "You're both equally bright young men. It's just that Rodney reads more than you do and pours a lot more information into his head."

After talking to his aunt, Wayne had felt a little better. He also vowed to read more books and start pouring more information into his own head. He started with *Treasure Island* but he could not get very far with it. Then he picked up *Huckleberry Finn* but could not

13

get very far with this book either. He kept reading the lines over and over again, because his mind kept wandering, and he could not stop thinking that there were three whole *Mighty Mike* comic books, which his friend Grover had lent him, that were still untouched on his nightstand—just lying there waiting for him—calling to him: "Hey, Wayne! Come read *me*! It's your pal, Mighty Mike! Who needs pirates and Tom Sawyer and all those…*words!*"

The Professor must have sensed that Wayne had lost some of his cheer, for he chucked him under the chin with his knuckles in a fatherly way and said, "If we succeed in our latest mission, I will treat the both of you to a hamburger at the Hungry Chef Diner." The thought of eating his favorite hamburger piled high with pickles and tomato and onion was just the thing to return Wayne to his former good mood, though his chin now smelled a little of sardines.

"Now let us take our stations, gentlemen, and put this baby into gear!" The Professor put Wayne at one end of the machine, which looked very much like a washing machine with knobs and dials in odd places, and he put Rodney at the opposite end. And he put himself at the controls. "Now boys, our implementation must be careful and gradual so that the pigment atoms detach themselves slowly and individually and do not affix themselves even harder through molecular trauma. Remember that when the frequency is potted all the way up, boys, the machine will begin to vibrate and then to shake quite fiercely and you must be quick about screwing everything back in before it all falls apart. Now we cannot have *that*, can we?"

Rodney and Wayne shook their heads as one. Rodney took a deep breath. Wayne steadied himself before the machine.

With a flip of the switch the Peach Pigment Evanescizer began to hum.

"It's building up steam," said the Professor. "Not real steam. That is just an expression."

The hum grew louder and then became a groan. The groan grew louder and then became a whine. The whine then became raised in pitch as if someone were playing a flute and taking the notes higher and higher. When the whine had reached a shrill screech it was hard for the twins not to drop their screwdrivers and Wayne to drop his canine earmuffs and throw their hands over their ears. (Wayne had considered putting on the earmuffs himself, but they were much too small to be wholly useful.) At that very same time the Evanescizer began to vibrate, just as the Professor had said it would, and now it looked like a washing machine in a different way, for it had begun to bounce and agitate as if someone had filled it with a load of heavy shoes. Gizmo decided quickly that she had had enough of the racket and went scampering out.

Within moments, the whole laboratory was shivering and shaking, and a long row of glass test tubes on one of the Professor's worktables began to tremble and clink and then one by one each of the test tubes began to *pop!* in just the way that crystal glasses shatter when an opera singer reaches a high note.

Wayne and Rodney watched as the Professor turned the frequency dial even farther in its clockwise direction, taking care not to pot it up too quickly. The sound rose even higher in pitch, and now other glass objects began to shatter all about the room, including the glass panes in all the windows! Rodney wondered if this would be the means by which the peach pigment problem would be solved—by destroying everything to which the color was attached!

A moment later the boys heard the sound of someone pounding his fist upon the Professor's back door. When no one went to open it, the door flew open on its own, revealing Officer Wall of the Pitcherville Police Department's Loud Noises Unit. Officer Wall stood with his hands over his ears shouting, "We cannot have this, Professor Johnson! No, no, no, sir! This cannot be! I will have to cite you! I will have to cite you!"

But the Professor paid Officer Wall no heed at all. He turned the dial even farther to the right, and then suddenly the high shrill screech gave way to silence. Or, rather, the machine moved to a frequency that could no longer be heard by human ears.

"Now, that's more like it!" said Officer Wall, enjoying the sudden quiet. He remained in the doorway, poking his fingers into his ears as if clearing his ear canals were a way to restore his temporarily-crippled hearing.

"Not done yet, Officer," said Professor Johnson from the control deck of the Evanescizer. The Professor had hardly gotten the words out of his mouth when a howling began in the next room—just as he had predicted. Then the howling moved into the laboratory, and there was the little dog that was doing it: the Professor's Scottish terrier Tesla. With one hand Wayne continued to screw in the wobbling screws that were working their way out on his side of the machine and with the other he tried to put the canine earmuffs around Tesla's head as he had been instructed to do. But it was not an easy thing to do because Tesla would not remain still. He kept running back and forth and wailing and complaining, and it was almost heartbreaking to see him in such a state. After a little struggle, Wayne finally succeeded in getting the muffs around Tesla's delicate ears, and it was no time at all before the little dog stopped complaining and sat down to study what the humans in the room were doing.

Unfortunately, the other dogs in the town of Pitcherville had no one to put canine earmuffs on *them* and so they all began to moan and howl and whimper and caterwaul and bark and some to growl in one great town-sized canine chorus. And then something very strange happened! Every dog that was able to get itself out of its house or yard took it to mind to come directly to the Professor's house, some perhaps to discover the source of their discomfort and put an end to it, others in obedient response to the loudest dog whistle they'd ever heard. A couple of old junkyard mutts who were deaf joined the large pack of dogs for the sheer fun of joining a large pack of dogs!

Together they stampeded through the gate that had been left open by Officer Wall, and then scrambled and tumbled right up to the back door and then right *through* the back door—all dust and fur and peach-colored paws and peach-colored muzzles and jangling collars and scruffy collarless ruffs and wagging tails and a few bared fangs. Right through the door they came, knocking Officer Wall completely off his feet. And down upon the floor *he* went, landing with a thud and then promptly becoming—against his own wishes—one very trampled human dog mat.

Within a moment or two, the laboratory was filled with yowling, howling, insistent dogs, all demanding in their dog-like way that Professor Johnson put an end to the hurtful noise that only they could hear, even as the noise had begun to do its job. You see, the sound vibrations emitted by the Evanescizer had begun to make the pigment detach itself from everything that it had affixed itself *to*—from Mr. Lipe's car and Mr. Edwards' car; from Mrs.

Carter's bruised head and Mrs. Wyatt's bruised head; from every tree and every mailbox and every tiny blade of grass; from all the dog muzzles and Tesla's canine earmuffs; from the cushions of the booth at the Hungry Chef Diner where the boys would soon be enjoying their well-deserved hamburgers; from all of Aunt Mildred's spice jars (each of which contained only cinnamon) and all the town's television antennas; and even from Officer Wall's Noise Complaint Citation pad, which was now stamped with muddy paw prints.

"Look around! It's working!" cried Rodney, as a Great Dane whined right into his ear.

"Another moment longer and everything will be restored to its natural color," said the Professor. "There will be tons and tons of pigment dust to be cleaned up from this town, but at least it won't be attached to anything."

"My bottom hurts," said Officer Wall, rubbing the place where he had fallen so heavily.

"Arf!" said Tesla, who seemed to like his noise-proof canine earmuffs and the company of all of his dog pals.

Gizmo, for her part, had retreated to the Professor's bedroom upstairs, where she was vengefully using one of his walnut bedposts as a brand new scratching post.

As Professor Johnson frequently liked to say: "There is always a price to pay for science."

CHAPTER THREE

In which the Professor's theory is shared with Petey,
the steel-head-plate boy, and explained to the reader as well

On their way to school the next day, Rodney and Wayne found their young friend Petey Ragsdale standing patiently next to his bicycle in his peach-pigment-dust-covered driveway. (It would be many days before all of the pigment dust was shoveled and bagged and put into the town dump.) The fact that Petey was waiting for Rodney and Wayne was nothing out of the ordinary, for almost every morning Petey joined the twins for the second half of their ride to school. Petey was only eleven and wished that he were older so he could grow a few inches taller and be the same size as his friends. Then other children would not make such fun of him (he was quite short, even for his age), and would not make equal fun out of the fact that one side of his head was covered with a large steel plate. The plate had been put there when Petey was eight and had had brain surgery. The surgery had been successful and the doctor had said that Petey should expect a very long and healthy life, but he should be careful when he turned his head in the bright sun or the reflection from the shiny skull plate would get in people's eyes and possibly cause a traffic accident.

Rodney and Wayne never made fun of Petey. They did not care that he was short or had a shiny steel plate in his head (which he usually kept covered with a baseball cap). They did not even mind that he walked around with a Cub Scout backpack so filled up with books and school supplies that it looked as if he were about to take a two-week hike. So the three boys became good friends, although it was sometimes hard for Petey to keep up with the twins. They generally ran faster and peddled faster and even talked faster than Petey, who was a bright boy, but had lost the part of his brain that understood the letter "*b*." This meant that words that had the letter "*b*" in them looked or sounded foreign to Petey, and would have to be replaced by other "*b*"-less words—not a big problem but sometimes a small inconvenience.

There was something very comfortable and familiar about the way that Petey waited for the twins every morning, and this morning was no exception. But this particular morning there was something different about Petey. He was holding a large object in his hands. As the boys drew closer on their bikes they could see that it was, in fact, a round cake, covered with peach-colored frosting.

Petey smiled. "This is from my mother. To thank you for saving the town from the invasion of the peach color."

"Petey—" said Rodney. "We can't take that cake to school with us, and there isn't time to get it back home. You'll have to return it to your mother and tell her that we'll be by for it after school."

"Okay," said Petey. "Wait for me."

Rodney and Wayne nodded.

While the two were waiting for Petey to come back out without the cake, a car slowed down and then stopped. It was a brand new aqua-colored Buick super sedan with white-wall tires, and it belonged to the father of Rodney and Wayne's friend and classmate Becky Craft. Becky sat on the passenger side of the front seat. She was waving at the boys even before she had fully rolled down her window.

Becky had straight dark brown hair and a round face, bright blue eyes and a button nose, and it was hard for Rodney and Wayne not to smile at her when she smiled at *them*. Becky was—generally speaking—a happy girl, though she had lost her mother at the very same time that Rodney and Wayne had lost their father. Mrs. Craft had been the town librarian, and she had been very good at her job. After she disappeared upon that fateful night when Rodney and Wayne's father and Professor Johnson's assistant had disappeared, the library was turned over to Mrs. Craft's volunteer helper Miss Joyner, who did not have the skills to be a good librarian. For example, Miss Joyner decided that it would be better to group all the books on the library shelves by the colors of their covers and spines. Conversations with Miss Joyner at the library usually went something like this:

"Good afternoon, Miss Joyner. I have to write about wool in my social studies class. Would you tell me where I could find a good book on wool? Or a good book on sheep or goats—the animals that give us wool?"

Miss Joyner would think for a moment and drum her fingers on her lips as if she were playing a musical instrument with them, and then she would smile and nod and say, "I have seen a book on natural animal fibers in the blue section. That's where you'll find it!"

And generally it would take the remainder of the day for the person to look at all the books with blue covers for one that was about wool and flax and other natural fibers. It would not be wrong to say that most library visitors greatly missed Mrs. Craft and her respect for the card catalogue.

"You have done it again!" said Becky to the boys. "You and the Professor have saved the town from another disastrous calamity."

"Yes, thank you, boys!" added Mr. Craft from behind the wheel of his new Buick. Mr. Craft had to tilt his head in a funny way to look at the boys through Becky's window. "I was worried that I would have a very hard time selling any of the appliances at my store. People want white refrigerators and white ovens. They don't want peach-colored ones. Which is why I am greatly indebted to you and Professor Johnson for keeping me in business."

Mr. Craft owned the largest appliance store in Pitcherville. The appliance business had been good to him and allowed him to buy a new car every year and to put his only daughter into nice clothes. It was sad not having Mrs. Craft around, but she was replaced by a gardener and a maid and a cook with the name of Smitty (though she was a woman).

"And to show my appreciation for what you have done, I have asked Smitty to bake you a cake. It is in the back seat, if you'll open that door and take it out."

Rodney looked at Wayne and Wayne looked at Rodney and neither knew what to say, for Mr. Craft wasn't Petey and could not be spoken to so frankly. Luckily, Becky came to her friends' rescue: "Oh Daddy! Do you really expect Rodney and Wayne to be able to take the cake *now*! For goodness sake! We'll give it to them later."

Mr. Craft smiled and shrugged. "You boys better hurry on to

school or you'll be late."

"See you in class!" chirped Becky, as the Buick drove away.

"What did I miss? What did I miss?" cried Petey. He had just come out of his house and was now running down his front walkway. Petey was always arriving after something had already happened or was just finishing up.

"Mr. Craft's cook Smitty made a cake for us," said Wayne. "Aunt Mildred is going to laugh when she hears that we now have two cakes on the way! That's three cakes in all, when you add the one that she's baking us herself!"

Petey climbed upon his bicycle, which, because he could not think about any words that had a "*b*" in them, he called his "Schwinn cruiser."

The three boys rode to school together on their Schwinn cruisers, Rodney wondering how in the world they were going to eat three whole cakes, and Wayne thinking about how lucky he was to have three whole cakes to eat.

At school, as they were rolling their bikes into the bike rack, Petey said, "My mother wanted me to ask you something."

"What is it, Petey?" asked Rodney.

"She wants to know if the Professor has told you how long these calamities are going to keep happening to the town. She said she doesn't trust the articles in the paper that say they come from sunspots. My mom is a nervous woman, and it makes her even more nervous not knowing what tomorrow has in store for us."

Rodney and Wayne both recalled the conversation they had had with Professor Johnson when the sixth in the long series of troubling events had occurred. This was the time that everything mechanical and electrical in the town began to run backward.

Clocks ran backward and cars ran only in reverse, and the boys could not get their bike wheels to go forward no matter what they did. (Mr. Dean, the editor of the town paper, the *Pitcherville Press*, had written an article—the latest in a long series of articles—which had repeated his belief that the mechanical and electrical problems that the town was experiencing were—like all the other calamities —caused by sunspots. Unfortunately, the very odd, bug-eyed and frizzy-haired editor could not get his printing press handle to turn in a forward direction; so he was left to stand at the window of his upstairs office at the *Pitcherville Press*, and shout the word "sunspots" at all the people who passed below as another means to get across his minority opinion.)

As Professor Johnson was working with Rodney and Wayne to build a Chrono-Gyro-Restorifier to correct the problem, he offered the finer points of his theory: "Pitcherville, you see, is an ordinary town that has apparently been picked to undergo a series of most extraordinary permutations. Hand me that number seven wrench, please. Do you boys know what the word 'permutation' means?"

"Changes," said Rodney.

"That's right. Different, um, *transmogrified realities*."

"'Transmogrified'—now what does *that* mean?" asked Wayne, looking in the toolbox for the right wrench.

"Well, it means changed but in a most bizarre way."

Wayne laughed. "Gee, that would be Pitcherville all right!" He handed the Professor the wrench he needed. "But why do you think that is, Professor?"

"Well, I've spent a lot of time pondering our situation. Why have we been singled out for such recurring calamities? Why, every few days, do the laws of science and nature stop applying to the town of Pitcherville? Why do things happen that are sometimes funny like everything being the color of lemons, and sometimes scary like the time that the town found itself entirely under water—like the lost ocean city of Atlantis—and all the electrical appliances shorted out? Why is this?"

"And what have you concluded, Professor?" asked Rodney, holding a bolt in place so that the Professor could put in the screw that it required.

"Here is my theory—and it is *only* a theory. The day that your father disappeared—that same day that Mrs. Craft and my assistant Ivan and two of the other professors from my college all disappeared—that was the day that the experiments began."

"Experiments?" the twins asked together in one curious voice.

Professor Johnson nodded. "You see, I believe that Pitcherville has become a laboratory of some sort. Just like this laboratory in which we're now working—just like my other laboratory at the college. But instead of being a place of beakers and Bunsen burners and vacuum tubes and electrical circuitry, it is a laboratory of houses and streets and trees and people. Of dogs and cats and cars and swing sets and tree houses and go-karts and television sets and electric razors and toasters and flower gardens and everything else that marks the lives of average Americans in this modern year of 1956. I believe, boys, that there is a force out there—the same force that took your father (for I cannot believe that the two things are not related)—which is responsible for these experiments. They—whoever they are—want to see how we react to each new situation."

"Like they want to know," said Rodney, "if we can live in a world in which everything that was once hard and solid has become like Jell-O and everything that was once soft and squishy has become hard and solid."

"Or if we can live in a world with millions of bubbles," added Wayne. "Or in a world where people speak in numbers instead of words. Isn't that right, Professor?"

"Right on the money, Wayne."

(Wayne smiled. He had been right on the money!)

"Of course those who are conducting these experiments, boys— they probably never realized that they would have Professor Johnson and Rodney and Wayne McCall to contend with. For every time a new experiment has been put into place, there we are—like flies in their ointment—busy at work on a new machine that will end the experiment and put things right back to normal!"

"Oh, I'll bet they're not happy about that at all!" laughed Wayne a little raucously. "And who cares!"

Rodney and the Professor could not help laughing along with Wayne. "Hand me those pliers, Wayne," said Professor Johnson with a chuckle.

Rodney's gaze now went to one corner of the laboratory where the Professor had been constructing a different machine. "How is the Force Field-De-Ionizer coming along?" he asked.

"Not as well as I would like. It is a most difficult thing to learn the make-up of a force field when it is invisible. And without a proper chemical analysis of the molecular structure of the field itself, I cannot hope to build a machine to remove it."

"And you believe," said Wayne, "that the force field, which keeps us from leaving Pitcherville, was put up by the same people who are doing the experiments on this town?"

"I do, Wayne. What better way to keep the guinea pigs of these experiments—*us!*—from escaping from our town-sized cage! Yet I am hopeful that it will only be a matter of time before I am able to solve the riddle of the force field. For is it not turned on and off at times and in certain places to send the radio and television signals to us? Or to place the things we need to survive upon the shelves of the town warehouse? Say, Wayne, what makes you think that it is *people* who are conducting these experiments?"

"Who else *could* it be?" asked Wayne, his eyes rolled upward in thought. "It couldn't be horses or—or elephants—or Venus Fly Traps doing this to us." (Wayne was fascinated with Venus Fly Traps and all other plants that had the ability to take revenge upon members of the Animal Kingdom, and so he sought whenever possible to bring a Venus Fly Trap into a conversation no matter how very much it did *not* have to do with Venus Fly Traps!)

"Did you ever stop to think that perhaps our experimenters might not be earthly at all!" posed the Professor.

"You mean that they could be Martians?" asked Wayne.

"Or maybe beings from some planet we've never even heard of before!" marveled Rodney.

"I have no idea who it could be. Perhaps we should start to gather the clues that will someday give us that answer. What, for example, do we know of our situation here besides the fact that we are subjected to these periodic calamities?"

Rodney thought for a moment and then said, "That we are cut off from the rest of the world."

The Professor nodded.

"And that we cannot send letters or make telephone calls to anyone who lives outside of Pitcherville," continued Rodney.

"And nobody calls *us*," sighed Wayne, "or sends *us* letters. Or birthday cards. Or Christmas cards or *anything*."

Rodney nodded and brought forth a sigh of his own. He was thinking of how much he missed his father and how the force field kept him from going to look for him. But it was not just their father whom the twin brothers missed; they also missed having a mother around—for Mrs. McCall had died when they were born. They missed all of their relatives who lived outside of Pitcherville whom they wondered if they would ever see again: Grandpa and Grandma McCall (who was the sister of their Great Aunt Mildred) and their Uncle Doug, who was a traveling magician, and even their father's friend Trixie, who was a dancer and would sometimes come to town and laugh too loud and get on Aunt Mildred's nerves. There were a lot of people whom Rodney and Wayne missed seeing and whom they would miss even more if they were destined to live the rest of their lives trapped in Pitcherville.

And there it sat: the Force Field-De-Ionizer all in pieces, because the Professor had little clue as to how he should put it all together in such a way as to do the town some good and remove its invisible fence forever.

"So that's the Professor's theory, Petey," said Rodney, summing things up. "And he could be wrong, but it sounds like as good a theory as any other that I've heard."

Petey agreed, and said that his mother would be glad to hear it. It would be good for him to give her a possible reason behind all the Troubles—to give her some theory that had nothing to do with sunspots (which few people believed anyway). But Petey said this using only words that did not contain a "*b*."

"Of course there is one other thing that Mom wants to know," said Petey. "She'd like to know when the next experiment is going to happen. She said she wasn't very prepared last time, and doesn't want that to happen again."

Rodney shrugged. "Sometimes we have two whole weeks between calamities," he said.

"But gee, other times," Wayne joined in, "there's hardly even time to take a good breath."

"A good what?" asked Petey.

"A good inhalation," said Rodney, thinking of a "*b*"-less word that means "breath."

The school bell rang. This meant that it was now time for all the children who had been talking and chasing one another upon the front lawn to go inside and begin their school day. Rodney and Wayne didn't hurry, for they knew what would be waiting for them in their classroom, and wanted a little time to prepare what they would say. And, of course, their guess was right on the money; there it was: a cake—a big peach-frosted cake baked by their teacher Miss Lyttle "to thank you boys and the Professor for ending yet another town catastrophe! Have a piece, boys. We'll wait to begin class until after you're done."

CHAPTER FOUR

*In which Rodney and Wayne wake to discover that they have been
sleeping like babies because they ARE babies!*

Nothing new happened for several days. Each morning Rodney and Wayne woke to a bright and sunny room, with nothing whatsoever out of place. Down to breakfast they would go to eat their cinnamon biscuits and their cinnamon-sprinkled grapefruit (which, though it sounded strange, actually tasted pretty good), and to gather their books for school, and then to jump upon their bikes. Petey would be waiting, patient as usual. Mr. Craft's aqua-colored Buick would pass the boys on its way to the school, and Becky would roll down her window and wave and sometimes she would shout, "Don't you love this good, beautiful, normal day!"

Some days the three boys were joined on their Schwinn cruisers by Rodney and Wayne's friend Grover. Grover was a stocky boy in the twin's eighth-grade class whose mother was Professor Johnson's housekeeper and cook, Mrs. Ferrell. Grover was always trying hard to lose weight. In fact, the Professor had built an exercise machine for him that was like no other exercise machine in the world. It was part rowing machine and part stationary bicycle, but also had a medicine ball that came out of its own accord and pushed at him here and there, which Grover had to fend off when he wasn't looking. He never used the machine without acquiring a bruise or two, and finally, the Professor was forced to concede that the "Grovercizer" needed further work. It was Grover's dream to lose weight and not have to shop in the husky young men's section of Lowengold's Department Store, but he would prefer to do it without acquiring bruises.

Grover hoped to grow up to be a champion wrestler like the wrestlers he saw on television. His favorites were Whipper Billy Watson, Bobo Brazil, Killer Kowalski, and Gorgeous George who preened and strutted in a silly way and made Grover laugh. Sometimes Grover would pull one of the twins down to the ground without warning and pin them and shout, "You're pinned! I win! I win!" even when the boys had not been aware that there had been a wrestling match in progress. But Rodney and Wayne could not help liking Grover, who, just like Becky and them, had only one parent, and who, just like the two boys, had never even met one of his parents. You see, Grover's father had died in the Battle of Guadalcanal in World War II. He had died a war hero, and Grover kept all of his medals in a little box next to his bed.

Rodney and Wayne spent their normal school days listening to their pretty, young eighth-grade teacher Miss Lyttle talk about the differences between reptiles and amphibians, and the differences between acids and bases, and the differences between Theodore Roosevelt and Franklin D. Roosevelt. And all of these non-calamitous days were generally good days, except that they were sometimes a little boring.

And a little bothersome. The bothersome part went by the names Jackie Stovall and Lonnie Rowe. These were two boys in Rodney and Wayne's class who had no friends other than each other. There was a very good reason for this: nobody liked them. And there was a very good reason why nobody liked them: they tried their best to make trouble for their classmates whenever possible. Lonnie liked to put out his leg and trip anyone walking past. (Most of the students in the class had learned to give him a wide berth.) However, Jackie's mischief was more cunning. He would think of things to hurt people that no one had ever thought of before. And it was not only children who were the victims of his naughty behavior. Sometimes he would steal the newspapers left by the paperboy in the early morning. (This would have a double benefit to Jackie; people would have to start their day in a sour mood without their *Pitcherville Press Morning Edition*, and they would blame the paperboy for not delivering it.)

Sometimes Jackie replaced the milk that the milkman left on the porch with milk bottles filled with soapy water. He was always careful to cover his tracks and pretended never to know anything when it was time to get to the bottom of something bad that he had caused. Once he slipped away from school and disguised his voice and called Principal Kelsey on a pay phone to tell him that he had better hurry home because his wife had left the faucet running in her bathtub before she left the house and there was a cascade of water coming out of his upstairs bathroom window. The absent-minded principal was halfway home before he realized that there was no upstairs floor to his house.

And that he did not even have a wife.

But Jackie Stovall reserved his most illustrious acts of mischief for Rodney and Wayne, because he was envious of the boys and all the good things they had done for the town through their work with Professor Johnson. Sometimes it would be a little thing like replacing the boys' bologna sandwiches with mud sandwiches. But sometimes Jackie's stunts were of a far more serious nature—like the time he put itch powder in the boys' costumes when they played Pilgrims in the school Thanksgiving pageant. Several people in the audience had watched the twins jumping and wriggling around on the stage and had pointed at them and laughed in a way that Miss Lyttle (who had written the Thanksgiving pageant herself) had not intended. One woman had said in a loud voice, "Those two Pilgrim men must have to go to the bathroom! Take those Pilgrim men to the bathroom, Chief Wahunsunacock!"

All went well for so many days that the citizens of Pitcherville began to wonder if the calamities had stopped altogether. "Wouldn't that be marvelous!" exclaimed Aunt Mildred, who was working late in her kitchen to make cinnamon fudge for Professor Johnson. (Aunt Mildred, you see, was quite fond of the bachelor professor and he liked her too, during those occasional moments when he could think of something other than his work.)

Then it happened: it was early in October when the mornings had gotten a little cooler and the leaves on the trees were just starting to show a little color that was not green.

Rodney woke, as he usually did, without opening his eyes, and knew that this was going to be one of *those* days. How did he know this? Because his arms and legs felt funny. They felt somehow smaller than usual. How could such a thing be? he asked himself, and do I dare to open my eyes to find out? Not only did his arms and legs feel funny, but his pajamas felt several sizes larger than they did when he went to bed. And where was his pillow? He reached about his head and could not feel it.

This is terrible, Rodney thought. I have been shrunk to a miniature size! Rodney had wondered when this might happen. Only a few weeks before, he and Wayne had sat down and made a list of all the different bad things that had yet to happen to the town of Pitcherville, and Rodney, remembering the problems of Alice in Wonderland, added to the list the possibility of everyone in the town being made very tiny. "And now it's happened!" he said aloud, his eyes still squeezed tight.

"Now *what's* happened?" Rodney had never heard this voice before—it was very high and very squeaky. And yet there was something a little familiar about it.

"Open your eyes, fraidy cat!" said the voice, now taunting him.

And this is what Rodney did. He opened his eyes and glanced in the direction of the voice—in the direction of his brother's bed—and there, sitting up against the wooden headboard that had been painted with a long wagon train, was a chubby baby of somewhere between one year and two years of age (Rodney was not good at telling the age of babies and toddlers since he didn't spend much time around them). The baby looked very much like Wayne had looked when he was very young, for it had taken at least two years for Rodney to gain some weight and Wayne to lose some weight and the two to look more like twins. This is the way it often is with identical twins: one is born bigger than the other, and it takes a while before they grow into their identical-ness.

The baby looked quite comfortable and casual sitting against the headboard. But he did not look entirely happy. "Will you get a load of this? I'm a baby!" he said in a not-very-happy voice. "And you're a baby too. And I would have woken you up sooner, but you were sleeping so peacefully. You were sleeping like a baby."

Rodney stretched out his little arms and stretched out his little legs and knew now for certain that he was a baby too.

"Has everybody in Pitcherville been turned into babies?" asked Rodney in his own high and squeaky voice.

Baby Wayne shook his baby head. "I don't think so. I heard Aunt Mildred a little earlier singing in the bathroom. I'm pretty sure she wasn't singing in a baby voice."

"But that doesn't make any sense!" said Rodney. "Usually, when a bad thing happens to the town, it happens to *everybody* equally."

At just that moment the boys could hear the bathroom door open.

"Now we'll find out!" said Wayne. "AUNT MILDRED! COME IN HERE!"

A moment later Aunt Mildred stepped into the room. She had a turban on her head made out of a bath towel. There was something very different about her that the boys could not put their finger on (besides the fact that she wore a towel turban—something they never remembered her doing before).

"I wondered when you were going to wake up," said Aunt Mildred cheerily. "You were both sleeping so peacefully. You were sleeping just like babies."

"Because we *are* babies. Look at us," said Wayne. "And why aren't *you* a baby?"

Aunt Mildred shrugged. She had a smile on her face that did

not go away.

"Why are you smiling?" asked Wayne testily. "Are you enjoying the fact that your great-nephews have been turned into babies?"

"I wasn't enjoying that at all! I was merely taking momentary pleasure in the fact that when I looked at myself in the mirror this morning, it seemed as if I had grown at least ten years younger!"

Rodney nodded. It was making perfect sense to him now. "Aunt Mildred," he said, "how old would you say Wayne and I look right now?"

"Well, if I can remember back to when you actually *were* babies, I would say you look as if you're about eighteen months old."

Rodney calculated aloud: "Wayne and I are around eighteen months old. Yesterday Wayne and I were thirteen years old and two months. That means that we have had a little over eleven-and-a-half years chopped off our physical ages."

"Oh don't say 'chopped,' dear. Say 'trimmed.' It's a much nicer word." Aunt Mildred could not help herself: she giggled. "And what an even more pleasant surprise for *me*! I'm not just *ten* years younger! I'm eleven-and-a-half years younger! Let me see. Oh goodness! I was sixty-five and now I'm fifty-three. And what's more, I don't look a day over forty-nine. Please note how soft and supple my skin looks now!"

Aunt Mildred pinched her cheeks so hard that they turned red.

Wayne's face now took on a pout. He looked like a baby who had just done a little business in his diapers. "Don't you even care that Rodney and I are now helpless infants?"

"Of course I care, dear. I care very much. But I'm not sure how helpless you are. Let's see if you can walk so I won't have to carry you around. But first, let's get you out of these giant-sized pajamas so you won't stumble." Aunt Mildred went to Rodney's bed and helped him out of his pajamas. He tried very hard with his little arms to be of some assistance, but his tiny hands would not do what his brain wanted them to do. After Aunt Mildred had removed the top and bottom halves of his pajamas, Wayne started to laugh. It was very much a baby's laugh, like a little baby giggle, but there was definite thirteen-year-old mirth involved. Mirth at Rodney's expense.

"What are you laughing about, you chubby baby!" Rodney squeaked.

"*You!*" answered Wayne. "Those underpants look huge on you!"

"And *you* don't have on huge underpants yourself?" Rodney shot back.

"I guess so," said Wayne sheepishly. "I guess we both look pretty foolish."

"Oh you look adorable!" said Aunt Mildred as she picked Rodney up and put him down on the floor. Then she went to Wayne's bed and began to undress him. Once the boys had both been set upon the floor, they attempted together to pull themselves up into a standing position by climbing their little hands up their bedposts. After some grunting and a great deal of effort, they got themselves to their feet. It was a good start.

"Now come *toward* me, boys," said Aunt Mildred, lowering herself to a squat. "Let me see if you are still babies or if you've reached the toddler stage yet."

Rodney took a step away from his bed and promptly fell down. Wayne took a step away from his own bed and then another step and then another, each one coming faster than the last, until he was hurtling uncontrollably toward Aunt Mildred, on a collision course with her bony knees. Just short of his great aunt's outstretched arms, Wayne toppled headlong to the floor.

"But that's a good sign, isn't it?" said Aunt Mildred, helping Wayne into a seated position and then clapping her hands gleefully together as if the boys really were babies who required encouragement. "It means that you just have to work at it a little and you'll both be up and walking around in no time."

Rodney scowled. "What are you *talking* about, Aunt Mildred?" he said through his tiny baby mouth. "We're not going to stay like this! I'm sure that the Professor is in his laboratory right this moment working on a machine to undo this. Can you take us to his house?"

"Right now? Right this very minute? But I have to get you some breakfast! I have to buy baby food! I have to go up into the attic and find your high chairs and find the double baby carriage that I used to roll you around in. It will take me all morning to get things ready for us to go to the Professor's house. Why don't I just call him up on the phone and have him come over?"

Rodney and Wayne looked at one another and shrugged. It probably *did* work better for the Professor to come there.

"Now crawl around if you like, but be careful and don't pull any table lamps down on your heads." (Aunt Mildred was always worried about things coming down on people's heads and giving them amnesia as was always happening to the characters in her favorite radio soap opera *Helen Grant, Backstage Nurse.*)

Rodney scowled anew. "Aunt Mildred, we might look like babies to you, but we're actually thirteen-year-olds who are merely trapped inside the bodies of babies."

Aunt Mildred nodded. "I must remember that it is our physical bodies that have gotten younger and not our brains, or else you would not be able to talk to me the way you are and would be drooling a little. Please forgive me, boys. But I must say, though: it is such a delight to see you so young and adorable again. I so hated it when you boys had to grow up."

"Yeah, yeah, yeah," said Wayne, trying his best to be agreeable, but still sounding like something the world had never before seen: a sarcastic baby.

From down the hall now came the sound of a ringing telephone. "Speak of the Devil! That could be Russell—I mean Professor Johnson!" exclaimed Aunt Mildred, clapping her hands together excitedly.

The now fifty-three-year-old Aunt Mildred who didn't look a day over forty-nine put her hand to her chest as if to slow her fast-beating heart. "I wonder what the Professor will look like! Quite dashing, I'm sure!"

Wayne and Rodney sat on the floor and stared at each other in silence as they listened to their aunt scampering down the hallway. Then they could hear her talking on the phone, although she was too far away for them to tell what she was saying.

"You just watch, Wayne," Rodney finally said. "I'll be running all around this house before the end of the day. By tomorrow the both of us will be hard at work in the Professor's lab, helping him to make this calamity go away."

"And how will we do *that*, Rodney? I can't even make my fingers work by themselves. Look. I'm trying to point at you, but all the fingers are pointing together."

"Then we have to train our hands the same way we will train our legs!" Rodney was trying to have a positive attitude, but it wasn't easy for him.

"At least I'm further along with the walking than *you*," said Wayne, beaming. Wayne was proud of the fact that he had just propelled himself across the room upon his own two legs while Rodney was still having difficulty taking his very first step.

Rodney looked around for something he could throw at Wayne to put him in his place. Seeing nothing that he could even lift with his small arms, he just sat and sighed until Aunt Mildred came back into the room. She was no longer smiling. In fact, she seemed quite upset.

"It's really quite terrible. I don't even know how to say it."

"Say it!" said Wayne. "Tell us what's wrong."

"Boys, that was Petey's father, Mr. Ragsdale. Petey is gone. He wasn't in his bed when everyone woke up this morning."

"But if Rodney and I woke up as babies, then Petey would have woken up as a baby too!" said Wayne. "Has he been kidnapped?"

Rodney shook his head sadly. "I can tell you what has happened, Wayne. How many years younger were we when we woke up this morning?"

"A little over eleven-and-a-half years was our estimate," said Aunt Mildred gravely.

"And how old was Petey yesterday?"

"He turned eleven in July," said Wayne.

"So Petey hasn't been kidnapped. It's even worse than that: he hasn't even been born yet!"

CHAPTER FIVE

*In which the Professor puts his head out a window,
Becky makes a mess in the kitchen, and a lost child places
an important telephone call from an undisclosed location*

Later that morning, Rodney and Wayne sat on the sofa in the room which their aunt called "the den" and which the boys called "the TV room," and which their father had nicknamed his "bear cave." Mr. McCall had given the room this name because it was the place where he watched all of his football games, roller derby matches, and championship boxing. This was the room in which Mr. McCall allowed himself to growl at the television and to be a grumbly bear when his favorite boxer or favorite football team did not perform their best. (Or when one of his favorite female roller derby skaters took a bad fall and eight other skaters skidded and tripped and landed right on top of her. Then the growl and the grumble would be replaced by a very loud 'OOOF!' or 'YOWCH!,' or 'MAN OH MAN, THAT HAS *GOT* TO HURT!'")

Outside of this room Mr. McCall wasn't much of a bear at all, but a soft-spoken man who made a quiet living writing books. Mr. McCall wrote serious, scholarly books about fairs and festivals and rodeos and circuses—any event in which people gathered together to throw balls at cans or watch animals do amazing things or observe people from other lands dressed in their native costumes.

When Mr. McCall was a young man, he attended the 1939-1940 New York World's Fair, at the time one of the largest world's fairs that had ever been staged. Mr. McCall later wrote a book about the New York World's Fair, and one could find within the den/TV room/bear cave many pictures and posters and souvenirs from the fair. The souvenir Rodney and Wayne liked most from their father's collection was a tabletop model of the fair's "Trylon and Perisphere." The model sat on a little table next to Mr. McCall's easy chair. The actual Trylon was a tall, pointy tower that rose into the sky like the Washington Monument. Its companion, the Perisphere, was so large in actuality that fair visitors could ride a long escalator right into the middle of it to find out what the "World of Tomorrow" was going to look like.

Becky's father, Mr. Craft, who sometimes came to the McCall home to watch boxing matches with Mr. McCall and Mr. Lipe and Principal Kelsey, once picked up the model of the Trylon and Perisphere and tossed it back and forth in his hands in a disrespectful way, and made a funny comment about it. He said that the real Trylon and Perisphere must have looked to people like a gigantic golf ball that had fallen off its gigantic golf tee. Mr. McCall was not amused. He stopped inviting Mr. Craft to the McCall home after that remark.

But this didn't stop Mr. Craft from returning to the McCall home on *this* particular morning. Here he was standing in the den holding his baby-sized daughter Becky in his arms. Mr. and Mrs. Ragsdale were also present. Mr. Ragsdale, looking very upset, kept running his trembling hand over and over again through his thinning hair. (Yesterday Mr. Ragsdale had been totally bald but now he had some hair.) Mrs. Ragsdale was wringing her hands and pacing alongside her husband. There were other worried people in the room as well, each looking about eleven-and-a-half years younger, and each of whom had come to crowd themselves into the small room to find out what was to be done. They had followed Professor Johnson all the way from his house to the McCall residence, peppering him with questions along the way: "What has happened to my little boy? Where did my little girl go?" People often turned worriedly to the Professor when a new calamity struck the town, but this time they were even more worried than usual, for there was the serious matter of lost children to be concerned about.

Mr. Craft had come on behalf of one of the salesmen at his appliance store, a man named Armstrong, who had that morning gone into the room where his six-year-old girl Daisy and his four-year-old boy Darvin slept, and found their beds empty. He was so upset that he went into the bathroom and climbed into the tub with all of his clothes on and would not get out.

Mr. Dean, the newspaper editor, had also come to the house. He wanted to hear the Professor's opinion about what had happened so that he could put it in his paper. Mr. Dean had already written the first few lines of his article about the latest calamity and was waiting for the Professor's comments so that he could finish it. In the article Mr. Dean planned to remind his readers that the most logical reason for the disappearance of Pitcherville's youngest residents was sunspots, pure and simple. But he had an obligation to give other possibilities, even if those other possibilities pointed to a Pied Piper or bad milk. It is the duty of a journalist to give all sides—even the ones that make no sense.

"So what *is* your theory, Professor?" prodded Mr. Dean. He rudely waved his reporter's pad in front of Professor Johnson's face as if he expected the Professor to write the theory down himself.

Professor Johnson pushed the pad away. He was feeling uncomfortable because he didn't like being trapped in tight spaces with a lot of people. He didn't ride elevators for this reason, and he never played games in which the object was to see how many people could fit into a broom closet or large crate.

"I do have a theory," said the Professor in an uneven voice. "It is the same theory as the one which my assistants Rodney and Wayne have come up with. Rodney, my boy, why don't you tell everyone our theory while I put my head out this window for a breath of air?"

Rodney explained to all the people in the room how he believed that eleven-and-a-half-years of instantaneous reverse aging had put those children under that age into a pre-existing state. And that was why they were nowhere to be found—for there were no bodies around for them to occupy.

"Then where *are* they?" sobbed Mrs. Ragsdale. "What has happened to them? Will I ever see my Petey again?"

Wayne stood up on the sofa, his legs bowing out like a baby's and making him a little unsteady on his feet. Both he and Rodney were now wearing the baby jumpers Aunt Mildred had pulled out of the attic cedar chest. The jumpers had a pattern of little ducklings and goslings on them. Wayne placed one of his hands on his hip and raised the other into the air as Mighty Mike might have done when he was a super-hero infant.

"The Professor is working on the problem," he said. "You can be assured that this problem will be corrected and all of your children will be returned to you. Isn't that right, Professor?"

The Professor did not hear the question. His head was still outside the window and he was making a sucking noise, trying to draw more air into his lungs.

Mr. Craft stepped forward and addressed Rodney and Wayne: "How can you be so sure that we will get the children back?"

Neither Rodney nor Wayne knew how to respond, and the Professor wasn't being very helpful. Before the boys could come up with an answer, the telephone in the kitchen rang. Aunt Mildred, who had been serving coffee to people, set down her coffeepot and went to answer it.

"You all must be patient," said Becky from the envelope of her father's arms. "The Professor is working very hard. Even harder than usual."

"No he's not," said Mr. Dean, the newspaper editor. "He's sticking his head out of the window."

"Well, if there weren't so many people in this room making things so difficult for him!" Rodney and Wayne had never seen their little friend so upset before. It was even more unusual to see her large baby eyes fired with anger and her rosy cheeks even rosier than they had been earlier. It was usually Becky's nature to be cheerful or at the very least, politely pleasant. But Rodney and Wayne could certainly understand the reason for this change in behavior. It wasn't easy being a thirteen-year-old girl trapped inside the body of a rubber-limbed baby. Becky had wanted to help Aunt Mildred make and serve the coffee to all of her guests, but there was very little that she could do with her flimsy, nubby baby hands except stack sugar cubes upon a saucer, and even then, some of the cubes wound up on the table and on the floor. Finally, Aunt Mildred was compelled to return her helpless little helper to the arms of her father and thank her politely while getting the whiskbroom and dustpan.

Aunt Mildred had been gone hardly a minute when she returned to the den with a puzzled look on her face. It was as if someone had told her the answer to a funny riddle, but it made no sense.

"What is it? What's the matter?" asked Mrs. Carter, whose ten-year-old daughter Lucinda had also disappeared the previous night. Mrs. Carter was perhaps the most worried parent in the whole room, because she had quarreled with her daughter before sending her up to bed without supper. They had quarreled over the fact that Lucinda refused to eat her raisin and carrot salad. Lucinda had even stuck her tongue out at it, and right in front of Mrs. Carter's friend Mrs. Edwards, who had made the salad herself and had tender feelings about it. Mrs. Carter was afraid that her daughter Lucinda had run away from home. For this reason, she had spent part of the morning standing on her front porch calling, "COME HOME, LUCINDA, MY LITTLE GIRL! YOU WILL NEVER HAVE TO EAT RAISIN AND CARROT SALAD EVER AGAIN. YOU ARE RIGHT! IT TASTED JUST LIKE RABBIT FOOD!" This last part was said just as Mrs. Edwards strolled by with her dog. It was a very awkward moment for both women who were already on delicate terms with one another after the head-bumping incident.

"Petey is on the phone," Aunt Mildred said.

"*Who* is on the phone? *Who*?" barked Mr. Dean, who had not heard the first part of the one-sentence report. Like a good news-paperman, Mr. Dean needed to know the "who," the "what," the "when," the "where," and the "why" of everything newsworthy that happened in the town.

Mr. Dean's raised voice drew the curious Professor's head back into the room.

Aunt Mildred turned to Mr. and Mrs. Ragsdale and said, "Your missing boy Petey is on the telephone!"

With that, the Ragsdales dashed out of the den and down the hall to the kitchen. Mr. Ragsdale yanked up the phone receiver resting on the kitchen counter, and Mrs. Ragsdale leaned in to listen alongside her husband.

"Where is your extension?" asked the Professor of Aunt Mildred as all the adults in the den went scurrying down the hallway to join the Ragsdales in the kitchen.

"There is one upstairs in my nephew Mitch's bedroom," said Aunt Mildred pointing to the staircase behind her and smiling because she could be helpful to the Professor.

"Thank you," said the Professor with a nod of the head. With his now more youthful legs, he was able to take the stairs two at a time.

In the den, Rodney and Wayne sat alone on the sofa thinking that they had been forgotten in everyone's mad rush to find out if it really was Petey Ragsdale on the phone and from where on earth he might be calling.

"HEY!" yelled Wayne. "SOMEBODY! ANYBODY!"

In an instant, the normally absent-minded Principal Kelsey, who had shown up at the McCall front door concerned about how his school children would be affected by this most recent calamity, swept into the room and scooped Baby Rodney and Baby Wayne into his arms. With a grunt, he said, "You might be eighteen-months-old, but you're still just as heavy as two sacks of potatoes!" Carrying the boys, one under each arm as if they were, indeed, potatoes, the school principal conveyed them to the kitchen, which was now just as crowded as the den had been, and for want of any better place, set them down in their old high chairs.

"Petey? Petey is that really you on the phone?" asked Mr. Ragsdale into the telephone receiver.

"Yes, Dad. It's me, Petey."

"Well, I'll have to admit that it certainly *sounds* like you. But how can I be sure that it really *is* you?"

"I have a metal plate in my head and the little toe on my left foot doesn't have a toenail."

"But everyone knows *that*, son. Tell me something that only Petey and his mother and father would know."

"I know!" offered Wayne from his high chair. "Ask him what he had for lunch at school yesterday."

Mr. Ragsdale nodded. "Petey, son, tell me what your mother put into your Hopalong Cassidy lunch carrier yesterday."

"I don't have a Hopalong Cassidy lunch carrier, Dad. I have a Roy Rogers lunch carrier."

"Yes, yes, you're right! A Roy Rogers lunch carrier. Now tell me what your mother made you for lunch."

"A round meat sandwich and a yellow monkey fruit and some root juice."

"Oh, that's right!" exclaimed Petey's mother. "I packed him a bologna sandwich and a banana and a bottle of root beer. It's Petey! Only Petey would have said it just that way without any 'b's!" Mr. Ragsdale held the phone receiver out for his wife to speak into. "Where are you, honey? Tell us where you're calling from."

"I don't know."

"You don't know where you are?"

"No, I don't, Mom."

"What does it look like?" asked the Professor, speaking on the upstairs telephone extension.

"It doesn't look like anything. Is that *you*, Professor?"

"Yes, it's me, Petey. Now try very hard to give us some kind of idea as to where you are."

"Okay. It's very foggy. And there are clouds."

"And vapor. Is there vapor?" asked the Professor, jotting the facts down in his pocket notepad.

"Yes sir. Vapor and clouds. Oh, and fog. And also some steam."

Mrs. Carter could not help herself. She cried out, "Is my girl Lucinda with him? Ask him if Lucinda is there!"

Mr. Ragsdale nodded. "Petey, Mrs. Carter would like to know if her daughter Lucinda is there with you."

"Well, it's not easy to see everyone. There is too much vapor and clouds and fog and steam. I *think* she's here, though. Let me ask. LUCINDA? LUCINDA CARTER, ARE YOU HERE?"

A tiny voice replied, "I'm over here!"

"Yes, Dad. Tell Mrs. Carter that she's here."

"What about Armstrong's kids, Darvin and Daisy?" asked Mr. Craft. "Ask about them."

"Did you hear that, Petey?" said Mr. Ragsdale into the phone. "Are Darvin and Daisy Armstrong there with you?"

"Gee, I don't know, Dad. I'll find out. DARVIN? DAISY? ARE YOU HERE?

"They're right here!" replied Lucinda. "I've got them with me."

"They're here too, Dad," said Petey. "Say, Professor, what's going on? What are we doing here? When do we get to go home?"

"We're just starting to put all the pieces together, Petey. I'm afraid it will take a little time to get everything figured out. Now, do you have the sense that you are in a room, son? Or out-of-doors somewhere?"

"There are no walls that I can see, Professor," answered Petey. "Not even a ceiling or floor. It's like we're all sort of floating in *space*."

"Most curious," said the Professor, making notes. "And how old are you, Petey? How old are the other children?"

"The same age we were yesterday, I guess. I can't see much of a difference in the way we look except that you can kind of see through us like we're ghosts or something."

"Ghosts!" Mrs. Ragsdale shrieked. "That can only mean one thing!"

"*Corporeal transparency* could have many possible causes," said the Professor in a calming voice. "Now, Petey, how did you find the telephone?"

"Gee, I don't know, Professor. It just sort of appeared. Hey, are Rodney and Wayne there? They're not here with me."

"Yes, Petey. They're here," answered Mr. Ragsdale. "But they've been turned into infants and I don't think they know how to talk on the phone."

"Yes we do!" said Wayne, offended by the put-down.

Mr. Ragsdale made a "shh" sign with his finger and his lips, and then spoke into the phone. "Thank goodness there are telephones wherever you are, son. Now you take good care of yourself until the Professor can put everything back the way it was."

"I will, Dad. In fact, I'm doing more than just taking care of *myself*. It looks like I'm the oldest one here. *And* the tallest. I've never been in a place where I was the oldest *and* the tallest. I guess it's up to me to look after all these children until we get to go home."

"That's a fine thing, Petey. You make your mother and me very proud."

Mrs. Ragsdale pulled the phone receiver over to her mouth so she could say something else to her son: "Is there a number there where we can reach you?"

"I didn't understand the first part of what you said, Mom."

"A *number*, Petey. A phone number."

"Yes, there's a phone here. I'm talking on it."

"No, you don't understand, honey." Mrs. Ragsdale began to cry. "Oh Drew—I can't think of another way to say 'phone number.' Is there another way to say it so that it doesn't have a 'b' in it?"

"I'm thinking, I'm thinking," said Mr. Ragsdale.

"I can hardly hear you, Mom."

"You're fading too, sweetie. But don't go yet! Don't go!"

"I love you, Mom! I love you, Dad!"

"We love you too, honey."

"So long!"

"So long, son."

Mr. Ragsdale handed the phone receiver back to Aunt Mildred and wiped a tear from his cheek.

A moment or so later, the Professor returned to the kitchen. A somber quiet had fallen over the room, with the exception of the scratchy sound Aunt Mildred made sweeping sugar into her hand from the messy table.

"There is a name for the place where Petey and all the other little children of the town are being kept," he said softly. "But Petey wouldn't have understood. The place is called 'limbo.'"

CHAPTER SIX

In which Rodney and Wayne and Becky and Grover have an encounter with two preschool fugitives from the law

The next three days were very busy ones for Professor Johnson and for Rodney and Wayne. Although they were not able to help the Professor with the construction of the invention—dubbed the Age Altertron—whose job it would be to end this latest calamity, the boys nonetheless spent as much time as possible with their friend in his home laboratory. They even helped him to give a name to the new calamity. It would forever be called *The Age-Changer-Deranger-Estranger.*

Aunt Mildred didn't mind rolling the twins back and forth between the two houses in their big double stroller because it gave her more opportunities to bring fudge and pie and all the other special foods that Mrs. Ferrell had told her the Professor liked. Aunt Mildred would sometimes sit and watch Professor Johnson bolt down a slice of cinnamon-rhubarb pie (so that he could quickly return to his work) and she would let out a little wistful sigh and wonder what life would be like if she could bake for him everyday as his wife. When it was time to go, Professor Johnson would steal a glance at Aunt Mildred through his window and think about what a good cook she was, and how much he liked to see the cheerful lift in her step when she walked.

Rodney and Wayne were busy in large part because the Professor's house and laboratory at 1272 Old Hickory Road had become a very busy place. All day long Mr. and Mrs. Ragsdale and Mrs. Carter and all of the other parents of the missing children (except for Mr. Armstrong who could not be coaxed from his bathtub) would drop by to find out if they would soon be able to hold their little ones in their arms again.

The Professor's students from the college, who had once been eighteen- and nineteen- and twenty-year-olds, and who were now seven- and eight- and nine-year-olds, came to visit with the Professor as well. Now that they had the bodies of young children, they could no longer while away their free hours doing the goofy, prankish things college kids generally did, like leading a milk cow up four flights of stairs to the roof of the science building. Now that they were incapable of doing anything more prankish than covering a very short tree with toilet paper, they could spend more time assisting the Professor in those areas of his work that did not require a steady adult hand.

In fact, there were so many people gathering at the Professor's house that he could scarcely get any work done. "I don't care how you do it, boys!" he had said to Rodney and Wayne on the third day of the calamity. "You simply must figure out some way to keep everyone away from here who isn't being helpful to me. It's a circus in this place and it only delays my work and hurts this town."

So, here is what Rodney and Wayne decided to do to help the

Professor: they set up a reception room in his front parlor. No one was allowed to go to the back of the house to see the Professor unless he or she had a very important and urgent reason.

"I have an idea!" said Becky, sitting with the boys and their friend Grover on the Professor's front porch. "Let's make it into a real office, like we have our own company. I'll be the receptionist and Rodney and Wayne, you can do the interviewing since you know better than anyone else whom the Professor would be willing to see and whom he would not."

"And what will *my* job in the office be?" asked Grover. Grover sat at one end of the funny row of chatting babies, each with serious faces and furrowed brows—faces usually only seen on babies with poopy pants.

"There are plenty of things you can do to help our brand new company," said Becky, who was convinced now that they should turn their work for the Professor into a fully-fledged business operation.

Mrs. Ferrell was watching the four chattering toddlers from the window of the Professor's front parlor. She smiled. She was pleased that Rodney and Wayne and Becky were including her son Grover in their plans. She had gotten very worn-out lately trying to tend to her chubby baby boy who was not content to simply sit quietly in a playpen and roll a toy car back and forth. At the same time, Mrs. Ferrell still had to cook and keep house for the Professor. She got so worn-out that sometimes she fell asleep standing straight up, propped against the Professor's dusty fireplace mantle.

"I know what Grover can do!" said Wayne. "Grover can be our right-hand man."

"What does a right-hand man do?" asked Grover.

"All kinds of odd jobs," replied Rodney. "Let's say, for example, that someone comes to see the Professor and won't take no for an answer. Well, it will be your job to show him to the door."

"But what if he doesn't *want* to be shown to the door?"

"Then you'll have to be forceful about it."

"But how can I be forceful?" asked Grover. "I only learned how to walk yesterday."

Rodney and Wayne and Becky all nodded at the same time. Slowly they had been learning how to walk all over again. Running and riding bikes and tramping through the woods and flying kites and playing football—all of these things were out of the question now. For the four children who sat in a little row that day upon the top step of Professor Johnson's porch, being so young had become a most cruel thing to be.

Not so, though, with the adults in the town. Being made younger worked very much to their advantage. Down the street at just that moment, Mr. Williford rode by on his son's bicycle, with his arms waving above his head. And there, directly across the street from the children was the butcher's wife Mrs. Garrison, taking a quick turn upon a sidewalk hopscotch court. And not too far away, the children could see Mr. Watts happily bouncing down the street upon his daughter's pogo stick.

"You would think by the way they're all acting, that they've all been turned into children again!" grumbled Rodney.

"Better children than little monkeys like you!" said someone coming from the Professor's side yard. The foursome looked down from the porch to see Jackie Stovall and his chum Lonnie Rowe snickering at them from the Professor's flower bed, where they had just trampled most of his autumn chrysanthemums.

Jackie and Lonnie, who had both been put back a grade, and were, therefore, a year older than the four sitters on the porch, had easily crept up on legs that functioned just as well as any older child's. (They did, after all, have the bodies of three-year-olds to work with.) Jackie was the taller of the two boys, but Lonnie had a strong, stocky build, like a young gorilla.

Becky stood up and said in the very serious voice of a no-nonsense receptionist: "Good afternoon, Mr. Stovall. Good afternoon, Mr. Rowe. Have you gentlemen come to see the Professor, because he is only seeing people with the most urgent emergencies."

"No, we don't have to see the Professor, monkeys!" crowed Jackie. "We just want to use his house for a hiding place. We're fugitives, you see. The law thinks we did something that we didn't do."

Rodney stared hard at Jackie and his fellow fugitive. He felt like a judge glaring down at a convicted criminal from his high bench. "What crime did you *not* commit that someone thinks you committed?" he asked in his official interviewer's voice.

"*Somebody*—really *two* somebodies—just ran through the Pitcherville City Park and overturned all the baby carriages. And there were about a dozen of them. Maybe more."

"Maybe *two* dozen," said Lonnie.

"How do you know?" asked Becky with a skeptical look. "Were you there?"

"No," snapped Jackie. "But that's what we heard. Two wild boys—oh, maybe just our size, went on a rampage through the park and knocked over about two dozen…"

"Maybe even *three* dozen," interrupted Lonnie Rowe, smiling proudly.

"Three dozen—shut up, Lonnie—three dozen baby carriages,

most of them with the babies still inside."

"Maybe *four* dozen," said Lonnie.

"I told you to…" Jackie suddenly took something from one of his little-boy-dungaree pockets that was floppy and black. He hit Lonnie over the head with it. "…to shut up," he concluded.

"Do they have a description of the rampagers besides the fact that they were about your size?" queried Rodney.

"Yeah, they were wearing black bandit masks."

"You mean like the black bandit mask you just hit Lonnie with?"

"Uh—uh—this isn't a black bandit mask. It's my black hand-kerchief. Isn't that right, Lonnie?"

Lonnie nodded. "Jackie likes black handkerchiefs because they hide all the dirty crud that comes out of his nose."

Jackie hit Lonnie on the head again.

"And for some strange reason," guessed Rodney, "the police think it's you two who did all that rampaging."

"That's right, monkey. Because whenever anything bad happens in this town, it's always Lonnie and me they point the finger at. So why don't the four of you be good little monkeys and stop blocking the stairs so Lonnie and I can find ourselves a good hiding place inside the Professor's house?"

"I don't think so," said Wayne sternly. Then he put one arm around his brother Rodney's shoulder and one arm around his friend Becky's shoulder, so that they could together make a better barrier against the two bully-fugitives.

But Jackie would not be deterred. He tried a friendlier tack: "Come on, you guys! I heard that the house had this great big basement, and there's an even bigger one beneath *that* one! Wouldn't it be swell to explore them?"

Wayne softened a little. "Two basements? One on top of the other?"

"Uh huh."

Wayne turned to his brother. "The Professor never told us he had a secret sub-basement!"

"*Waaayne!*" Becky pursed her lips. She squinted her eyes and gave Wayne a scolding look.

"I don't care if the Professor has basements going all the way down to China, Jackie, you can't come into his house," said Rodney sharply.

Jackie fixed his lips into the beginnings of a snarl. "I bet you'll let us hide out in this house after I get finished slugging you with this fist, monkey." The smarter and louder and more self-confident of the two bullies took a menacing step toward Rodney, his fingers already curled into a fist. Just as suddenly, though, his fingers relaxed.

"No, no. I'm not going to use my fist. I'm going to use my head. Just like my old man does to get what *he* wants. I can't wait until I'm as old as he is and then I can be mayor myself and all you monkeys will have to do what I say!"

Jackie had hardly finished speaking when the squeal of a whistle pierced the air. "Uh oh," said Lonnie, who wasted no time in running off.

"This isn't over, monkey," threatened Jackie from over his shoulder as he raced off in the same direction as Lonnie.

The foursome on the porch watched as the two partners in crime disappeared behind a neighbor's dwarf fruit tree, which had toilet paper all tangled up in it. Then they watched as two police officers ran up the cobbled walk from the sidewalk. One of them kept going in the direction that Jackie and Lonnie had gone. The second of the two officers stopped. He was very winded and gasping for breath. "Don't—stop—Stillwell!" he called to his partner between gasps. "I'll—catch—up with—you—in a—minute!"

The officer looked up at the children on the porch. "I have asthma," he wheezed. "It's better than it used to be, but it's still with me, unfortunately."

Rodney and Wayne knew the police officer well. Officer Wall used to work in the Pitcherville Police Department's Loud Noises Unit but was now detailed to a brand new police unit that had been created to handle an outbreak of toddler crime.

"So did they really go on a rampage and knock over all the baby carriages in the park?" asked Wayne, with interest.

Officer Wall nodded. "It was a real war zone for a while—all these carriages toppled over and all the babies yelling and cursing and shaking their fists. I think this was the intent of the masked troublemakers—to stir up a bunch of trouble, and that's exactly what happened next. All these infants and toddlers and pre-schoolers started running around having tantrums and kicking and biting and lobbing pine cones at one another from behind their overturned strollers. The problem is—it's been four days now and there are a lot of you kids who used to be teenagers who aren't having a good time being reverted in your ages, and it's all getting out of hand. Then you have troublemakers like Jackie Stovall and Lonnie Rowe who agitate. They agitate, that's what they do."

"You said it was like a war zone?" asked Wayne, who was trying to picture what all the chaos and destruction must have looked like.

Officer Wall nodded glumly. "Do you know where the word 'infantry' comes from?"

Four heads shook "no" together.

"From 'infants.' Makes sense, doesn't it? I'm not kidding you, kids. I can't wait for this thing to be over. I want to go back to my old job in the worst way."

"That's all you've been doing lately—stopping fights between children?" asked Rodney.

"Yes. Although I couldn't help issuing a few loud noise citations for some of those bawling babies. They're little human foghorns, that's what they are. Oh, I've also been investigating a robbery over at the Gun and Knife store. Somebody took several revolvers from a display case. *And* ammunition. It had to be one of you little people, because there was no sign of forced entry. We think it was somebody small enough to crawl through the ceiling ductwork. You wouldn't happen to know anything about this, now would you, kids?"

"No sir," said Rodney respectfully. "Although I have a good idea who it *might* be." Rodney darted his eyes in the direction that Jackie Stovall and Lonnie Rowe had run, to give the officer a good hint.

"Don't think that hasn't crossed my mind. Jackie has been a thorn in the side of the Pitcherville Police Department since he was old enough to start running over people's feet with his tricycle. I don't know why Mayor Stovall hasn't done a better job of reining in his son. Now you kids be good and don't you go and get yourselves mixed up in any of the craziness that's going on out there."

"We won't," said Grover. "Besides, we can hardly even walk."

Officer Wall tipped his hat and went off to find his partner. Rodney and Wayne agreed with Becky when she said that it was turning out to be a very interesting day.

CHAPTER SEVEN

*In which a fateful decision must be made
and Rodney and Wayne are asked to help make it*

That afternoon, Rodney and Wayne and Becky and Grover, inspired by Becky's suggestion, all agreed to set up their business, which they named *Calamity Solutions, Inc.* Wayne built a receptionist's desk for Becky out of a large cardboard box. He also found a nursery room chair that she could sit in.

Wayne and Grover had just started to put together another desk for use when there were interviews to be conducted, when the front door opened and into the parlor walked a man in his thirties accompanied by a teenage girl. The man was familiar to the foursome but the teenage girl was not.

"Hello, children," said the man, shaking hands with each of the employees of Calamity Solutions, Inc. "Do you know me? Do I need to tell you who I am?"

"You're Mayor Stovall," said Rodney, who had been busy writing interview questions like "What is your level of urgency on a scale of one to forty-five?"

"If you are looking for your son Jackie, Mr. Mayor, we don't know where he is."

"Well, to be honest, I *have* been looking for him, ever since the first hours of this latest change to our town. But what else is new? My son is like a dusty sun beam that cannot be swept beneath the rug. And now I hear that he is in trouble again. But there is something more important that I have come to talk about. May we see the Professor?"

"But I don't know who your companion is," said Rodney, indicating the teenage girl with a nod of his head.

The girl grinned and then winked. "You don't know?"

Rodney shook his head. Becky and Grover shook their heads. Wayne said, "But I feel like I've heard that voice before."

"What if I were to say: 'And now Wayne McCall will lead us all in the Pledge of Allegiance.'?"

Wayne had been trying to cut out a place for legs in the cardboard box desk, using a pair of blunt children's scissors. He was having trouble holding the scissors the way they should be held, but he was determined not to give up. Now the scissors dropped from his hands. His jaw dropped too. "Is that *you*, Miss Lyttle?"

"It *is* me! Look at me! I look just the way I did when I was sixteen. Sweet sixteen. And my eyesight is so good I don't have to wear my glasses anymore. Isn't it wonderful, children? Do you know what I did yesterday? I helped two of the other teachers from our school lead a milk cow all the way up to the school roof. It was hilarious!"

Wayne didn't know what to say to this. Neither did his companions.

The Mayor's face now took on a serious, all-business look. "We have a petition we would like to present to Professor Johnson, if you would be so kind as to—"

"A petition?" interrupted Rodney.

"Yes," said Miss Lyttle.

"Well, I will have to interview you first. No one sees the Professor until an interview is given. Now, as you can see, I don't have an interview desk yet, so if you will follow me over to the Professor's sofa, we will proceed."

"He is very good at this," whispered Becky to Wayne.

"Yeah, yeah, yeah," said Wayne, rolling his eyes.

"Now," said Rodney, struggling to pull himself up onto the sofa.

"Would you like me to give you a boost?" asked the Mayor.

"No. That will not be necessary." Rodney continued to try very hard to pull himself up, but his little arms were too weak. He finally decided to conduct his interview from the floor.

"Now, what is the nature of your petition, Mr. Mayor?"

"We'd like the Professor to cease work on the machine—what is it called?"

"The Age Altertron."

"Yes, yes. This Age Altertron he is building. We would like for him to stop."

"Why would you want to do that?" said Rodney.

"Because there are some people who—how shall I put this?— who are receiving some benefit from the way things now stand. Let us take Miss Lyttle, for instance. She likes being sixteen again. She has more energy and more—more—"

"*Verve,*" said Miss Lyttle, trying to be helpful. "I have much more verve now. Also, my vision is 20/20 again!"

"Thank you, Miss Lyttle. Now let us take myself, for instance. About the time I turned forty I began to develop a little arthritis in my hands and a little rheumatism in my back. It has only gotten worse with age. With my body clock being reversed, both of my ailments have vanished. So, you see that for some of us, there is great benefit to what has happened to this town. Perhaps it would not be fair to *those* people to restore things to the way they were before."

"Tell him the other reason, Mayor," said Miss Lyttle, who was still smiling. She was, no doubt, still thinking about how hilarious it was to take a milk cow up to a roof.

"Yes, tell Rodney—and *me*—the other reason," said the Professor, who had just stepped quietly into the parlor.

"Hello, Professor," said Mayor Stovall, standing up and extending his hand to shake. "I'm so glad you decided to take a break from your work." Professor Johnson took the Mayor's outstretched hand and shook it formally and without pleasure. "And you know Miss Lyttle, the children's teacher, I believe."

"Hello," said Miss Lyttle, blushing a little.

"So, you have given the first reason why you want me to stop my work on the Altertron. Now give me the second," said the Professor.

The Mayor took a deep breath. "Well, we have a theory—see, we non-Professor types have theories too."

"Go on."

"And our theory is this: whatever unknown party is responsible for all the things that happen to this town, whether it's for good or bad—"

"Mostly bad, Mayor. But go on."

"Well, we theorize that perhaps they are merely waiting to deliver a change to this town that we will agree to. And if we agree to that change, for example, this turning back all of our body clocks by eleven-and-a half years—"

"Eleven-years, eight months, one week, four days, and thirteen hours to be more precise. However, I cannot be exact to the very minute and second without further calculation."

'Yes, yes," said the Mayor, taking out a handkerchief to blot his perspiring forehead and neck. "Well, our thinking is that the— um—unknown party, whatever it is—might be happy that we've found a change we like. And if that is the case, why, they might just go and leave us alone. It is worth a try, don't you think? Especially since the other way—the constant building of new contraptions to undo new challenges—well, *that* doesn't seem to be working all that well, does it? Just think, Russell: no more peach town or lemon town or bubbly town, or talking in numbers or having flippers for hands. No more of any of those things. Wouldn't it be wonderful to finally be a normal, average American town again? And perhaps they will even remove the force field and then I'll be able to take my family to Hawaii for a vacation. And who knows? Maybe Jackie will become a Hawaiian and decide not to come back home!"

The Mayor laughed at his own joke, but no one joined him.

"And what happens to all of the limbo children?" asked the Professor. "Will *they* ever get to go to Hawaii, or will they have to live the remainder of their days in a cloud?"

Miss Lyttle raised her hand as if she were one of her more enthusiastic pupils. "I would like to say something. I would like to suggest that your time might be better spent, Professor, using your scientific abilities to find the missing children, rather than working on this silly machine."

"It isn't silly!" exclaimed Becky.

"Not only is it not silly, it's probably the best way we have to bring our friend Petey and all the other missing children back to Pitcherville," added Rodney.

"And do you feel that way too, Professor?" asked Mayor Stovall. Professor Johnson nodded.

"Then I will have no choice but to put it to a town vote. And since the voting age in Pitcherville is twenty-one, I have no doubt that we will win, because it is the older citizens of this town who have the most to gain by leaving things the way they currently are."

"And when do you intend to have your vote, Mr. Mayor?"

"Well, today is Tuesday and we must properly notify everyone and get the ballots printed. I see no reason why we shouldn't be able to hold this vote by Thursday."

"So that gives me two days to finish my machine."

"You would do best to suspend your efforts now, Professor," said the Mayor matter-of-factly, "and go and get some rest. Who knows how long it will take you to finish your invention, if ever?"

"I will nonetheless try," said the Professor gloomily. "I owe it to the lost children to at least do that much. Good day to you both." Grover tried to open the door for the Mayor and for Miss Lyttle but he couldn't reach the knob. So he stood beside the door with his arm in the air as if he were giving them permission to depart.

As Miss Lyttle passed, she said, "I hope in eleven or twelve years after we have grown back to our former ages, I'll see you all in my class again."

"And *I* hope it's even sooner than that. Like maybe *Friday*!" shouted Wayne, who then added under his breath, "you cow hater."

Then they were gone. Professor Johnson dropped into a chair

and began to massage his temples. "I'm so tired," he said in a soft, sad voice.

"I wish there was some way we could help you," said Rodney.

"You've all been most helpful by keeping people from interrupting my work. But I had to come out here to see what was important enough to bring the Mayor to my home. I'm sorry now that I ever left my laboratory. However, it is good to know where things stand."

"You are doing the right thing," said Becky. She toddled over to the Professor's chair so that she could pat his hand to soothe him. Professor Johnson's hand was long and bony just like Abraham Lincoln's. The Professor gave her a smile, then patted her tiny hand in return. He gave his own knees a strong slap and rose with a groan from the chair. "There is much work to do."

Without saying another word, the weary Professor shuffled slowly and heavily back to his lab.

Late the next night, Aunt Mildred came into the boys' bedroom. A ringing telephone had awakened them, but in their groggy state they believed they had dreamed the sound. Just as they began to drift back off to sleep, their aunt spoke.

"Boys, it's Professor Johnson on the line. He wishes to speak to you. I will hold the phone up so you can both hear him."

"Hello, Rodney. Hello, Wayne." A dark, melancholy tone infused the Professor's voice. "I'm afraid that I have some sad news to report."

"Yes, what is it?" asked Wayne, speaking for both of the boys.

"I won't be able to finish the machine before the vote is taken tomorrow. I have already heard how the vote is leaning and it looks quite bad."

"Oh dear, dear, dear," said Aunt Mildred, who was listening in.

"I have always said that my machines should not be engaged without proper and thorough testing."

"That's right," said Rodney.

"Yet I haven't enough time left to test this one in order to guarantee its success. Therefore, I must make a fateful decision: do I go ahead and flip the switch tonight and cross my fingers and hope that something good will come of it, or do I throw in the towel and walk away?"

"What is the *bad* that might come from it?" asked Rodney.

"Who knows? Perhaps the machine will just sit there and do nothing. Or perhaps something will happen that we can't predict. That is the risk. Now here is the question: is it worth the risk—the chance for us to bring Petey and the other children back? To restore this town to the way it was?"

"You are asking *us*?" said Wayne.

"Yes. I am seeking the opinion of my worthy and trusted apprentices in the field of cataclysmic science. Should I flip the switch and pray for a positive outcome?"

Rodney and Wayne considered the question while their aunt did a little praying herself, right then and there.

Then Rodney said, "Yes, Professor. I think you should do it. And here is a reason you might not have thought of yet: let us say that you decide not to turn on the machine tonight. Then the town will take its vote and more than likely you will lose. They will ask you not to work on the machine anymore. But what if you decide later to disobey them? What if you can't help yourself and you find a way to work in secret? And what if someone finds out? Someone who voted against you. Maybe there are people who are just waiting to catch you working on the machine so they can throw you in jail or close down your laboratory or maybe even do both. Then what happens when another calamity hits our town? And you have no way to help? Because I don't believe the Mayor's theory that doing nothing will make all the calamities stop. Whoever is doing this to us doesn't like us very much. They took my father. They took Becky's mother, and your assistant Ivan. They will keep doing these things to us. Just you watch. And you won't be able to help us. And Wayne and I are still too young to do anything on our own. So there is the other reason why you should flip the switch tonight. Because if you don't, then things could get much, much worse."

"And what do *you* have to say, Wayne?"

"Ditto to everything that Rodney just said."

"You have nothing more to add?"

"Just one more thing, Professor. I would like to say 'Good luck, Professor Johnson.'"

"Thank you, Wayne."

CHAPTER EIGHT

In which Petey comes home, Becky makes a confession, and Rodney and Wayne lay claim to the same Hawaiian shirt

That night Wayne dreamed he was in the jungle and had come upon a massive boa constrictor. The snake was friendly at first and did not bite him, but Wayne remembered from a science report he once wrote about the world's largest snakes that boas do not generally bite. They *constrict*. After a while the boa grew tired of being friendly and decided to slither up to Wayne and do some constricting. The enormous snake twined itself around Wayne's arms and chest and thighs. It tightened its vise-like hold upon him, and in no time at all Wayne couldn't breathe. He's going to suffocate me! he thought in his dream, as he thrashed back and forth in bed.

At the same time that Wayne was being squeezed by one of the largest snakes in the world, his brother Rodney was having a nightmare of his own. He was also being squeezed. But it wasn't a snake that was doing the squeezing. In fact, Rodney couldn't see the agent of his trouble. Invisible hands were pulling invisible sashes to make his clothes tighter and tighter. Rodney wondered, is this a madman's straitjacket I'm wearing?

Usually, with nightmares that become *too* frightening, the brain will end the story by waking the dreamer up. Now both boys woke, almost in the same instant. They realized that the boa constrictor and the tight straitjacket-like clothing had been figments of their dreams. But if this were so, why didn't the squeezing they were feeling go away?

The answer was simple. Rodney and Wayne looked down to see that their toddler's pajamas, which had a pattern of cowboys and cowgirls on them, were straining with great difficulty to contain their bodies, which were suddenly much too big for them. Rips appeared in the chest and arms, and big tears ripped through fabric in the legs of the pajamas. It was as if both boys had grown up so fast inside their miniature P.J.'s that there wasn't time even to take them off!

Wayne switched on the lamp that sat on a little table between the two beds. His eyes grew big. "Rodney, look at us! We aren't babies anymore!" He ripped the left-over pajama-top fabric so that he could breathe better. Then he looked down as his chest.

"Rodney! Lookit! I have hair on my chest!"

Rodney tore apart his own pajama top and looked down to see that he had hair upon his chest as well. "And my hair is gray," Rodney noted.

"So is mine," said Wayne. "Bring your face to the light, Rodney, so I can see it better."

Rodney leaned into the dim light of the lamp, which had leather fringe around the bottom to make it look like a cowboy lamp. "Your face, Rodney—it's kind of old-looking."

Both of the boys' heads looked gaunt and narrow in the temples, and furrowed in the forehead. The cheeks and jowls were wider and puffier, as cheeks and jowls often become with age.

"How old?"

"Well, look at mine. How old do you think *I* look?"

"About the Professor's age, I guess. Probably a little older."

"How old is the Professor?"

"Well, Aunt Mildred baked him a cake for his birthday in February and she wouldn't put candles on it because she said it might burn the house down."

"That doesn't tell us how old he is, Rodney. Will you wake up and think?"

Rodney chewed on his lip for a moment. "I know that his birthday is February 29. It's the leap year day that only happens every four years. And this year—1956—is a leap year, which means that the Professor has to be an age that is divisible by four. And so I believe he is either sixty or sixty-four or sixty-eight. I would say sixty-four."

"Do you think we're in our sixties too?" Wayne felt the top of his head. "Hey, Rodney, I still have some hair."

"But it's pretty gray."

The boys grew silent, each pondering their new predicament. Then Rodney said, "I think the Professor has added too many years to everyone's ages. Instead of adding eleven years and eight months to put us back to where we were, he added over sixty years."

"Why would the Professor do that?"

"I'm sure it wasn't on purpose, Wayne. Remember that he said he wasn't certain what might happen when he turned the machine on."

"What does that mean, Rodney, for the town?"

Rodney thought about this for a moment. "Well, I would guess that if all those years have been added to *our* true ages, then all those years have also been added to *everybody's* ages. That means we now live in a town with a whole lot of really old people."

"You mean like the Professor? Like Aunt Mildred?"

Rodney nodded.

"How old do you think Aunt Mildred is now?"

"115. Maybe 120."

"Gee, that's pretty old, Rodney. I hope she isn't dead."

"Me too. Let's go find out."

The two boys who now had the voices and bodies of men in their sixties, got out of bed and, without stopping to find some clothes, raced to their great aunt's bedroom. The door was shut. They knocked. They waited.

Then Wayne said to the door, "Aunt Mildred? Aunt Mildred, are you still alive?"

"Don't ask her if she's still alive," said Rodney. "Don't ask people questions that can only be answered one way!"

"But that's the way I want her to answer it. I want her to say 'yes.'"

"Well, she isn't saying anything. And she didn't say anything when we knocked, either. We'd better go in and check on her."

Wayne opened the door, and the boys stepped inside. "Turn on that reading lamp," said Wayne, pointing to the standing lamp that Aunt Mildred used to read her romance novels and her issues of *Ladies' Home Journal* in her comfy arm chair. Rodney switched on the lamp. It cast a dim light around the room. But it was enough light for Rodney and Wayne to see their great aunt lying in her bed.

"Get a little mirror," said Wayne. "We should hold a mirror up to her mouth, like they do in the movies, to see if she's still breathing."

"I have a better idea," suggested Rodney. "I'll take her pulse." Rodney reached under the blanket and gently pulled out Aunt Mildred's arm. It was very thin and scored with veins that ran up and down it. The skin was loose and blotched with dark age-spots. Rodney took the wrist between his fingers and felt for a pulse.

"Nothing."

"Nothing?"

"No—wait. There's a beat. Okay, where is the next one? There's another one. Her heart rate sure is slow."

"Probably because she's the oldest person in the world, Rodney! But this is good. She isn't dead."

Just then, Aunt Mildred opened her eyes. Calmly, she looked at the boys and said in a small and feeble voice, "Hello, Rodney. Hello, Wayne. Is it morning yet?"

"No, Aunt Mildred," said Wayne. He looked at the Big Ben alarm clock that sat next to the bed. "It's just a little past midnight."

"What's wrong? Why are you two out of bed and why do you both look like middle-aged men?"

"Because we *are* middle-aged men, Aunt Mildred," said Wayne. "Rodney thinks that we must be in our sixties. Say, is that middle-aged or old?"

"It depends on whom you ask, dear," said Aunt Mildred. She spoke in a breathy, slightly labored voice. The boys leaned in to hear her better. "If you are thirteen, then someone who is in his sixties could be considered quite old. But if you are as old as I feel right now, sixty-something could be considered quite young."

"Well, you probably feel old, Aunt Mildred, because you're 115, maybe even older," said Wayne bluntly.

"Oh."

"Although that isn't your real age," added Rodney.

"I know that, dear. My mind is just as sharp as it's always been. It's my body that feels worn-out. Oh my word! I just thought of something."

"What is it, Aunt Mildred?"

"My friend Mrs. Craddock at the Shady Rest Nursing Home—I knit socks for her and take her chocolate pudding—she must now be as old as one of those big ancient tortoises at the zoo. Maybe older!"

Rodney and Wayne nodded, not knowing how to respond. Wayne thought how strange it was that his great aunt should be talking about reptiles when he had just been dreaming of them. Sometimes Wayne's mind wandered to things that were slightly off the subject at hand.

"Well, let me rest, boys, and then in the morning, you will have to serve me breakfast in bed, because I don't think I have enough strength to go down to the kitchen. I would like something easily digestible. And don't forget the cinnamon." Aunt Mildred closed her eyes.

"I'm going to the Professor's house," said Wayne.

"Right now?" said Rodney.

"I have to find out if he's all right."

"I'm sure he's fine," interjected Aunt Mildred drowsily. "If he's like me he probably just wants to sleep."

"But I don't think we should wait until tomorrow, Aunt Mildred."

Aunt Mildred didn't respond. She had fallen back to sleep.

"I suppose you're right about checking on the Professor,"

whispered Rodney to his brother as he closed the door behind him. "We'll only toss and turn and worry the rest of the night. But we should first try to reach him on the phone."

The boys used the telephone in their father's bedroom, happy to call someone without assistance. Wayne let the phone ring a dozen times but the Professor didn't pick up.

"Now I'm *really* worried," he said.

"Let's go over there," said Rodney.

The two boys walked to their father's closet and began looking for shirts and pants and shoes that they could wear, since all the clothes in their own closet were sized for thirteen-year-old boys. "I think we are now the same size as Dad," said Wayne, just as Rodney pulled out his father's favorite Hawaiian shirt. It was yellow and had pineapples on it.

"Hey, do you remember this shirt?" asked Rodney, holding the shirt up to show his brother.

Wayne smiled. "I sure do. Dibs!"

"You can't call dibs on something that's already in the custody of another person."

"That shirt isn't in your custody, Rodney. It's still on the hanger."

"And I'm holding the hanger, goofball."

"So, do you want to wear Dad's Hawaiian shirt, Rodney?"

"Uh huh."

"But I want to wear it too…and it's still on the hanger…and I said dibs."

"You're such a goofball, Wayne. My hand touched it first. That's what counts."

"Can we rock-scissor-paper for it?"

"No."

"So, go ahead and put it on, if you want to wear it so bad."

"Okay."

"Go ahead."

"Okay."

"Go right ahead."

"No, I changed my mind. *You* go right ahead. Here."

"No, I don't want to wear it. *You* wear it."

"No...I don't think so."

The boys grew silent. They were both thinking about their father, about how much he liked this particular shirt, which was the shirt he often wore when he was out trimming the hedge or washing his pride and joy: his two-toned blue and white 1955 Ford Fairlane. (This was a special memory of Wayne's; he loved cars just as much as his father did, and was additionally crushed to learn that the Fairlane had disappeared right along with his dad.)

Wayne reached out and touched another of their father's shirts. It was a polo shirt—the shirt he liked to play golf in. Now they saw their father's fishing shirt, with a lure still hooked to one of its many pockets, and the brown and white striped shirt he sometimes wore to his office where he wrote his books. Rodney had said that the vertical stripes made their dad look like a football official. "Better that than a convict!" laughed Wayne, thinking of the stripes going in a different direction.

Wayne sniffed. He smelled a scent in the closet that he knew, the scent of Mitch McCall's aftershave. It was almost as if Mr. McCall was right there in the closet handing the boys his clothes to wear.

In the end, neither Rodney nor Wayne wore the Hawaiian shirt. They found a couple of old shirts and pants from the back of the closet. These were clothes their dad hadn't worn for many years, and they didn't carry such strong memories for the boys.

On their way to the Professor's house Rodney and Wayne noticed something very odd about many of the other houses up and down the street. They all had their lights on. Perhaps the same things were happening in these houses that had happened in the McCall home: children suddenly catapulted into middle and old age, older family members suddenly made very old and frail and unable to rise from their beds. There would then be urgent telephone calls between concerned relatives and concerned friends. And people would go to each other's houses and drink lots of coffee and shake their heads and say "tut, tut" and "can you believe it?" and try to make some sense out of this latest calamity. It would end up being a very long night for many of the families of Pitcherville, just as it was proving to be a very long night for Rodney and Wayne.

For one thing, the back door that led into the Professor's lab was locked.

"That's funny," said Rodney. "Professor Johnson hardly ever locks this door."

The twins took turns knocking, but no one came to answer the door. Wayne began to feel guilty. "What if he hears the knocking and he's too weak to make it down the stairs?"

"Well, there is only one thing we can do now, Wayne. We have to get a house key from Mrs. Ferrell."

On their way to the Ferrell house Wayne said, "I wonder if Petey's back."

"And all the other children," said Rodney. "Say, Petey only lives a block away. Let's go over and make sure that he's okay too."

As Rodney and Wayne suspected, the Ragsdale house had all of its lights on, like the others. Rodney rang the doorbell. After only

MARK DUNN

a moment an old woman, perhaps in her eighties, answered the door.

"Hello? What is it? Who are you?" she said.

"It's Rodney and Wayne."

"Oh my goodness! You are grown-up men. Rodney and Wayne—you won't believe it! I've got my Petey Weety back! Petey! Petey! Come see who's here! It's your friends Rodney and Wayne McCall. They're all grown up just like you!"

Petey came to the door. He was completely bald. This fact made his steel plate stand out even more. Petey's face had aged, but standing next to his mother he did not look so terribly old. Besides the plate in his head, there was another reason Rodney and Wayne were able to recognize Petey rather easily, even though so many years had been added to his age. It was his smile. Petey Ragsdale smiled wide. Sometimes his smile would stretch all the way across his face.

"Hi Rodney. Hi Wayne. So I guess this is what we'll look like when we're old."

"I guess so," said Rodney. "Welcome home."

"How did you get home?" asked Wayne.

"No idea. One minute I'm trying to get some sleep in that crazy cloud place. It was really hard since there was never anything to sleep on. You just float. Then the next minute—kazam! Here I am on the floor of my room and there's a pain in my side and my neck aches."

Rodney and Wayne remembered that their friend liked to sleep on the floor of his bedroom like an Indian. While this was an easy thing for an eleven-year-old to do, it would not be recommended for a man in his sixties.

"Still, it's great that I'm home. Look at Mom. She's a lot older now. She doesn't look it, though, does she?"

Mrs. Ragsdale blushed. "That is what I've missed about my Petey Weety! He always says the sweetest things!" Mrs. Ragsdale reached over as if to tousle her son's hair. But since he didn't have any, she pulled her hand back and looked a little embarrassed.

"Come in, boys. We are celebrating Petey's return. We will do that for a while and then we'll spend some time being appalled at what had to happen to bring him home. But for right now, let's all be festive!"

Mrs. Ragsdale led her two guests into the living room. Sitting on the sofa were two old men and a woman who appeared to be in her sixties. Rodney knew immediately who was who. "Hello, Mr. Ragsdale," he said. "Hello, Mr. Craft. Hi Becky."

"Hi," said Becky. She had a strange look on her face, which made it hard to tell how she was feeling about what had just happened to her. Her hair was gray and she had pronounced crow's feet about her eyes. She also had some folds in her neck that were similar to those starting to show on her mother's neck before she disappeared, although Becky's were deeper.

"Becky is very happy, aren't you, Becky, that all the little children are back?" Mr. Craft patted his now sixty-something-year-old daughter on her knee. He did this slowly and stiffly as old people will sometimes do things, as if moving too quickly or fluidly was either an impossibility or was to be avoided because of the chance of injury.

Becky nodded.

"But this last hour hasn't been easy for her."

Becky shot her father a disapproving look, which told him to be quiet.

"I'm sorry, pumpkin," said the very old Mr. Craft, whose face was creased with too many wrinkles to count. "I wasn't thinking. So boys, did you hear that Mr. Armstrong is out of his bathtub now? He came out the minute his little Darvin and his little Daisy showed up. Of course they aren't so little now, but he was glad to have them, and they were all so glad to be reunited with each other that they all climbed right back into that big empty bathtub as a family and just hugged and hugged on each other."

"That's so nice!" said Mrs. Ragsdale as she poured the coffee. "Would you like some coffee, Becky?"

"No, I don't drink coffee," said Becky curtly. "Maybe you've forgotten, but I'm still thirteen years old. Thirteen-year-olds don't usually drink coffee. Thirteen-year-olds are hardly even teenagers. Oh, I just hate this! I absolutely hate it!"

Becky ran out of the room. The room was quiet for a moment except for the sound of Mrs. Ragsdale pouring coffee. Then Becky returned, wiping her eyes. "I'm sorry. I'm better. This is very hard. If the Professor isn't able to fix this, then we will lose a huge chunk out of our lives. I won't get to be a pediatrician who makes children laugh with her hand-puppets."

"You wanted to be a pediatrician! With hand-puppets! Oh how nice!" said Mrs. Ragsdale.

"You can still be a puppet-performing pediatrician, pumpkin," said Mr. Craft to his daughter.

"No I can't, Daddy. It's too late. It's too late to be anything now but old. I hate this. Why do things like this have to happen?"

"We don't know, Becky, but all is not lost." Mr. Craft looked at Rodney and Wayne when he said this. "Is it, boys?"

Wayne shook his head. "We were just going over to see the Professor."

"And ask him what needs to be done to fix things," said Rodney. "Would you like to come with us, Becky?"

Becky wiped her eyes with a handkerchief and nodded. "Maybe the walk will do me some good."

CHAPTER NINE

*In which the Professor berates himself, and a supermarket is robbed
of all of its soft food, the reason to be revealed later*

Walking in the bright moonlight, Rodney and
Wayne and Becky and Petey (who had decided
that he would like to come too, to thank the
Professor personally for rescuing him from the cloud place, even
though he was now prone to arthritis) kept to their own quiet
thoughts for a while. It was nice to be able to walk again, even though
the no-longer-youthful muscles in their legs felt tired and tight.

It was a strange thing to be strolling along so late at night,
bathed in the light of a moon that looked no different from every
other full moon they had known since they were first told by their
parents what that giant, bright orb was doing so high in the sky. It
was strange to be moving down a sidewalk whose every crack they
had counted and tried to avoid (lest they break their mothers'
backs), past all the trees they had climbed and from whose branches
they had hung down like monkeys, past familiar green lawns, now
browning in the change of season, past the same cars and hedges

and mailboxes and stop signs, and past the same Halloween decorations—scarecrows and Jack-o-lanterns that came out too early every year. It was as if nothing had changed, although a great deal *had* changed. And a great deal had been lost. Each child wondered as Becky had wondered: would they ever get it back again?

"I didn't know that you wanted to be a children's doctor," Wayne said to Becky.

"Who works with puppets," noted Petey.

Becky shrugged. "I thought you would make fun of me, the way we used to laugh when Dr. Kelsey would forget where he put the knee thumper or his stethoscope."

Becky's three companions smiled as they remembered Principal Kelsey's equally absent-minded brother who was a pediatrician.

"But then, Wayne, I remembered that you once said you wanted to be a space cadet like 'Tom Corbett, Space Cadet,' on TV, so I thought it was okay to tell you something that *I* didn't have much of a chance at either."

"Why did you think that I couldn't grow up to be a space cadet?"

"Because there isn't such a thing as a space cadet," said Becky. "Being a space cadet is a made-up job. Just like Tom Corbett is a made-up character."

"You don't think some day there will be astronauts, Becky?" posed Rodney. "Astronauts who will pilot their spaceships all the way to the moon and back?" Rodney glanced at the moon as he said this.

"Or to distant planets?" asked Petey, also looking at the moon but with a starry-eyed gaze.

"I suppose," said Becky. "But by then, we'll probably all be too old to go."

The children walked on for a moment thinking quietly to themselves. Then Wayne broke the silence. "I wish that some day Professor Johnson would make a freezing machine that could put a person into a big ice cube and keep him there until after all the calamities are over and the force field is down, and then thaw him out when things are much better than they are now."

"How do you know that things will be better in the future?" asked Becky.

"Well, don't things *usually* get better? We don't live in caves any more, do we?"

Becky could not hold back a smile. She was thinking of Wayne wearing a wooly mammoth fur, with a bone through his nose. "I guess you're right about that."

The four turned a corner and stopped. There was the Ferrell house with all of its lights turned on. And there, sitting on the porch swing, was a large middle-aged man. The man was mostly bald. You could tell this because his head was bowed and the top was all that you could see. It was moving up and down a little as if he were crying.

"What should we do?" whispered Becky to the others.

"Well, I guess we should first find out who he is," said Rodney. "He might need our help."

"I hope no one has died," said Becky.

"Excuse me," said Wayne, approaching the house. The man looked up. Wayne and the others could tell immediately who the man was. It was their friend Grover, many years older.

"Who is it?" asked the middle-aged Grover. He was squinting at the moonlit lawn and wiping his eyes with his knuckles. "I can't see very well. I think I need glasses."

"It's Wayne. And here is Rodney and Becky and Petey."

"Hi Petey. Welcome home," Grover said, taking a handkerchief from his pocket to blow his nose with. "I—uh—guess I'm getting a cold."

"I'm not feeling all that well myself," said Petey. "I woke up with arthritis."

"Come up here. I am just sitting here thinking about things."

"What are you thinking about?" asked Becky.

"Mama mostly. Suddenly she's very old. Is this a new calamity?"

Rodney shook his head. "No. I think it was the Professor's machine—the Age Altertron—that did it."

"Well, whoever or whatever did it, Mama now has to take very tiny steps when she walks. It took her three-and-a-half minutes just to get from her bed to the bathroom. How will she be able to clean and cook for the Professor? She'll lose her job and then we'll both have to go to the poor house."

"Grover, the same thing is happening to half the citizens of Pitcherville," said Rodney. "My Aunt Mildred can't even get out of bed. Something will have to be done to help *all* of the old people until Professor Johnson can fix this problem."

"How do you know that the Professor can fix it?" asked Grover. "How old is he now? He must be at least one hundred!"

"Well, I think he's actually older than that," said Rodney. "But if he is like Aunt Mildred, his mind will still be sharp. Maybe he'll have to work slower, but I don't think things are hopeless. We're going to his house now. We need your mother's key."

"I'll get it."

Grover got up from the porch swing. He had been a large boy. Now he was a very large man. The floorboards of the porch creaked loudly as he walked across them.

At the same time that Rodney and Wayne and Becky and Petey and Grover were mounting the stairs in Professor Johnson's house to gently wake the Professor, a robbery was taking place at Toland's Supermarket. The two perpetrators, each of whom wore black eye masks to conceal their identities, and each of whom held shiny new revolvers in their hands, had surprised the store's night watchman, Mr. Roessler. He had been dozing in a chair in the produce section and woke to the sound of something large being hurled through one of the front glass doors of the store.

As he tried to wake up and get his bearings, Mr. Roessler was approached by the two bandits. It was at this moment that something disturbing came to his attention—something even more disturbing to sleepy Mr. Roessler, the night watchman, than the fact that his employer's store was being robbed. He was *old*. Very old. And very tired.

Even if he hadn't become suddenly very old and very tired, there was little that Mr. Roessler could have done to protect the store, since Mr. Toland, Sr., the owner of Toland's Supermarket, didn't believe his night watchmen should be armed. As a result of this policy, all that Mr. Roessler could do now was stand with his trembling hands up in the air, and hope that the intruders wouldn't shoot him.

Each of the two masked men carried a large duffel bag over his shoulder. Mr. Roessler wondered from the size of the duffel bags how much money the masked men were hoping to steal from the store that night.

"This is a stick up," said the taller of the two men.

"I can see that," said the night watchman. "But I should tell you: I don't have the combination to the office safe. I don't even have a key to the office. I'm just here to chase away all the mice who come out at night to nibble on Mr. Toland's fruits and vegetables."

"We don't want *money*, Gramps," said the tall man. "Do you think we would have brought these duffel bags if we had wanted *money*?"

Mr. Roessler shrugged. "I just figured you were being optimistic."

"Why don't you just be quiet, you stupid old man?"

"I *do* look old, don't I? It's the strangest thing. I *feel* old too, but I'm only thirty-three. So what *have* you come for? Why are you pointing those guns at me?"

"Direct us to the cereal aisle, Gramps. My partner and I will be taking all the oatmeal, Cream-of-Wheat and other soft cereals you have."

"But I don't understand," said the night watchman. "There are fresh T-bone steaks and rib-eyes in the meat section. If I were robbing a supermarket that's what *I'd* take."

"And that would make you stupid-times-ten, old man. Now show us to the cereal aisle, and when we're done there, take us to where you keep the Jell-O and soft custard. And you'd better be quick about it, if you know what's good for you."

Mr. Roessler did as he was told, and stood by as the two masked men filled their duffel bags with all manner of soft food, and then disappeared into the night.

)

"Professor? Can you wake up, Professor?" asked Becky.

"Tap him again," said Wayne. "Tap him harder."

"Well, I'm not going to *hit* him, Wayne. He's in a deep sleep. We'll just have to wait for him to wake up."

"We can always wait, of course," said Rodney, "but then again, Wayne and I are his apprentices. This is what he called us last night: his trusted and worthy apprentices in the field of cataclysmic science. And as such—"

"That isn't what he called us," interrupted Wayne. "He called us his worthy and *trusted* apprentices. You got it backwards."

"My point is…"

"You don't have to tell me your point, Rodney," said Becky. "I'll shake him a little harder."

"That won't be necessary, Miss Craft," said a groggy Professor Johnson, opening his eyes into thin slits. "I am awake now and more than willing to bring you all up to speed. But first, Rodney, tell me who these other people are, crowded around my bed. And if you will all take a step back from this bed, I should be able to breathe a little better."

Everyone took a step back to give the Professor more breathing room.

"Well, it's Wayne and me, and Becky, of course. And that large man over there is Grover. And that smaller man over there is Petey Ragsdale."

"Oh, Petey! It's nice to see that you have come down from the clouds. How were you transported here? You must make detailed notes that I can put into my log. Write down everything you can remember about the experience."

Petey nodded.

"Well, hello to the rest of you children. Of course, you're no longer children any more, thanks to me. Someone help me sit up in bed. I haven't much strength."

Grover and Wayne helped the Professor prop himself up in his bed. "Thank you, boys. I could sleep another twenty years. Just like Rip Van Winkle. Of course, the result would be the same as what has just happened, wouldn't it?"

"Give or take about thirty years," said Rodney.

"Yes, I see what you mean. You're all looking a bit long in the tooth. Well, blame me for it. *I* did it. I was right there to see the end-product of my stupidity. My punishment started immediately, for I could hardly get myself up all those stairs. You see, I have now only a small fraction of the energy that I used to have. And I must have a little rest for all the days of work that lie ahead. By my calculation I am now in possession of the body of a one-hundred-and-seventeen-year-old man."

"Wowee!" said Petey.

"And what would that make *us*?" asked Wayne.

"Let me see," said the Professor. "You were all born in 1943, is that correct?"

"Our birthdays are all within six months of each other," said Becky with a nod.

The Professor did a calculation in his head. "Then you would all be around sixty-six-years old, give or take a few months."

"I'm *sixty-six*?" asked Becky with a look of distress.

"But you don't look anywhere near that age, Becky," said Wayne.

"Thank you, Wayne. That was sweet," said Becky, who was beginning to resign herself—at least for the moment—to her present state of "Age Change-Derangement-Estrangement."

The Professor heaved a heavy sigh of fatigue. "I suspect, though, that none of you will be able to guess *why* the machine has added so many more years to our physical ages."

Rodney and Wayne shook their heads.

"It was my fault—entirely my fault. I wasn't thinking. I suppose it was because I was too tired. I had two pieces of paper. On one piece I had written 'eleven years, eight months, one week, four days, thirteen hours, ten minutes, *and* forty-five seconds.' That is how much aging would have to occur to restore us all to the age we were at the moment when the original age reduction occurred. On the second piece of paper I had jotted down 'sixty-four years, seven months, two weeks, one day, three hours, fifteen minutes and fifty-eight seconds.' That was my exact age at the pivotal moment of the age reduction. You see, I had been using my own age as a base variable to calculate the constant that represented the difference between the 'before' and the 'after' of our ages. I accidentally inputted this second figure—my age—when I was setting the coordinates for the machine."

Rodney looked at Grover and Petey who were both scratching their heads. "In other words," explained Rodney, "instead of having eleven-and-a-half years added to our ages, the machine added sixty-four-and-a-half years."

"That's right. Due solely to human error. *My* error. It was a disastrous, numskull mistake that will now have grievous consequences for us all."

"What kind of consequences?" asked Grover, who did not like the word "consequences" even when the word "grievous" wasn't attached to it.

"Well, you no doubt see them all about you, already. There is no one left in this town now who is below the age of fifty-two. There are no more children—no more spry young people to give our town energy and vim and, and..."

"Verve?" asked Grover.

"Yes, verve. There are, conversely, people now living among us— if you call lying in a bed and sleeping for most of the day *living*— who are as old as 153—for I know of at least two residents of Shady Acres Nursing Home who had already passed the century mark."

"But I don't understand, Professor," said Wayne. "It seems like a pretty easy thing to fix. You just go back down to the lab and enter the correct age coordinates and 'Wham! Bam! Allakazam!' We're all back to our right ages again."

"If only it were that easy, Wayne," sighed the Professor. "But unfortunately, as I found myself in the midst of that rapid aging process a little while ago—a process that was wholly unexpected, and which startled me immensely, well, I let out a most frightening shout of dismay. Right there in my laboratory I screamed like a terrified little child. And the intensity of this unexpected eruption from my vocal cords surprised Gizmo, my cat, who had been sleeping soundly next to me, and she sprang into the air in that way that cats sometimes do, in which all their limbs become extended and all of their claws protracted, and she came down not upon that same spot on the floor in which she had uplifted herself, but she came down—I am sorry to report—right upon the back of my poor terrier Tesla, protracted claws and all, and a most terrible row between those two ensued.

"I reached into the fray to break them up, and in so doing I lost my balance—for this is the way with people of advanced years: they sometimes lose their equilibrium and stumble and fall—and I did so in a most inconvenient and destructive way! For I fell directly into the Age Altertron and jangled loose its circuitry board and caused a little unintended arcing between its electrodes, and this produced a little fire, which grew into a slightly bigger fire, and before I knew it, I was spraying my arcing, flaming, smoke-belching Altertron with a fire extinguisher. And when the smoke cleared and all the extinguisher foam had dissolved away, there was nothing left before me but a broken, wrecked shell of what that machine had once been—a testament to fatigue and stupidity and the tendency of dogs when attacked by cats to defend their canine honor at all costs.

"Everyone was counting on me and I let them down. I let *you* down." The Professor shook his head and closed his eyes and became very quiet.

Rodney and Wayne and their friends exchanged looks of concern. "You didn't let us down, Professor," said Wayne.

"No," agreed Becky, "you just made a mistake. Everyone makes mistakes."

"We just have to build ourselves a brand new Age Altertron— an Age Altertron II!" said Rodney with forced cheer.

"How long do you think that will take?" asked Wayne.

Professor Johnson opened his eyes. "You boys will have to be the ones to build it. Under my direction, of course. Because I am much too weak and frail to do anything but to tell *you* two what to do. Do you think that you can do it?"

Rodney and Wayne nodded.

"Excellent. Then all is not lost. But first, let me sleep, for I am very tired. I must have twenty-four hours of rest to recuperate. While I am sleeping, boys, go down to my laboratory and take an inventory of all of the parts of the wrecked machine." (Yawn.) "Set aside those which you think we can reuse and throw out those you think we cannot." (Yawn.) "And feed Tesla and Gizmo their breakfast." (Yawn.) "And tell your mother, Grover, that she isn't to overly tax herself at her now-advanced age, and may come to my house to cook for me only when she feels she is able." (Yawn.) "For that matter, I cannot eat much solid food in my present state anyway, but will be nutritionally satisfied with some oatmeal or Cream-of-Wheat or some other form of soft cereal or custard. If my cupboard is bare, then please go to Toland's Market, Grover, and procure soft foods that I can gum. Goodnight, children. I will speak to you again in twenty-four hours."

CHAPTER TEN

*In which Jackie Stovall finds his voice
and a worthy mission*

"So there it is," said Rodney, using one of his father's favorite phrases.

"Yes, there it is," said Wayne in agreement.

The two boys stood in the Professor's laboratory surveying the damage from the stumble and the fire. It was morning now, and Grover and Becky and Petey had gone home to rest. "We should get back home ourselves and make breakfast for Aunt Mildred," said Rodney, stepping over Gizmo, who was crunching her cat food. In the other corner of the laboratory Tesla was eating dog kibble, but keeping a wary eye on his now-mortal feline enemy. "Let's stop at the market and pick up some food that Aunt Mildred can eat."

The boys passed the Professor's key rack mounted on the wall next to the door to the garage. A special key chain hanging there caught Wayne's eye. He stopped and pulled it down to give it a closer look. The key chain dangled from a woman's head sculpted in metal. The woman's hair was flowing straight back as if she were facing a strong wind. "Hey, look at this, Rodney! It's just like the hood ornament on the Professor's car."

"That's because the key chain is probably made by the Nash Car Company. Put it back, Wayne. We have to get to the store."

"Why can't we take the Professor's Nash to the store? He won't be able to use it any time soon."

"Because it's the Professor's car, not your car. Put the key chain back."

But Wayne didn't obey his brother. Instead, he opened the door to the garage and turned on the light. There sat the Professor's 1946 Nash Ambassador convertible. Even though it was ten years old, the car looked as if it had just rolled off the car lot. It was black and sleek and outlined in glistening chrome. Like most of the cars of its day, it was sloped and curved as if it had muscles. The tires had white walls to them that had not even the slightest smudge of dirt.

"Isn't she a beauty?" said Wayne. "I'll bet the Professor has someone come in to clean and polish her every month."

"I'm not going to let you drive the Professor's car, Wayne."

"But I'm sixty-six years old!"

"*No*, Wayne."

"But Dad let me drive his Fairlane."

"Yes. Around the parking lot at the supermarket."

"But Rodney! That's exactly where we're going! To the parking lot of Toland's Supermarket!"

"Absolutely not, Wayne." Rodney snatched the key chain out of his brother's hand. "The Professor has enough to worry about without you demolishing his car."

"Then I'm just going to sit in it."

"Aunt Mildred is probably really hungry, Wayne. We have to

get to the store." Rodney pushed his brother out of the way so he could close the door to the Professor's garage. He returned the Nash key chain back to its hook on the key rack.

"Did you see how the grillwork shined, Rodney? How do you get grillwork on a car to shine like that? Say, Rodney, have you ever seen so much shiny front grillwork on one car?"

"You think about cars too much, Wayne. We have a lot of other things to think about right now."

Wayne nodded. He reached up and longingly touched the Nash key chain. Then he touched the two keys hanging from the chain, one of which would start the engine of his favorite car in the world—a car he wasn't allowed to drive, even though he was now sixty-six years old.

When Rodney and Wayne got to the supermarket, they noticed something strange. There was a small crowd of people gathered outside. Most of the men and women were either the same age that Rodney and Wayne now were, or a little older. One of the men looked like a grown-up version of Davy Rockwell, a boy in Rodney and Wayne's class at school.

"Is that *you*, Davy?" asked Wayne.

"Yeah. Is that *you*, Rodney and Wayne?"

The brothers nodded. Wayne was about to comment on how different they all looked, when Davy called out to the people around him, "Hey, lookit, everybody! It's Rodney and Wayne. Hey guys, how come we went from being babies to *this*? What happened?"

"Yeah, what happened?" asked Sharon, a blond-haired girl in

Rodney and Wayne's class who now had streaks of white running through her hair.

Before either of the twins could answer, a boy named Virgil, who had been the president of the Eighth-Grade French Club and always liked to use a little French when possible, said, "So I'll get to be a thirteen-year-old again soon, no? N'est pas, mon amis?" ("Is it not so, my friends?")

Rodney didn't want to tell everyone that it was on account of the Professor's accident that over fifty years had been added to everyone's ages. So he said, "The Professor is working on the problem. We are hopeful that things will be back to normal in no time."

Then Rodney turned to Davy. "What are all these people doing out here? Is the store closed?"

"Kind of. It's closed to anybody who needs to buy food for their really old family members."

"What do you mean?" asked Rodney.

Before Davy could answer, a man holding a megaphone stepped up onto a wooden citrus crate. Everybody turned to look at him. The man looked about seventy-five or so. He also looked like Mr. Toland, Sr., the owner of the store.

"May I have your attention please! Quiet, please!" shouted the man through his megaphone. "For those of you who do not recognize me, I am Henry Toland, Jr. As you can see from this door, we had a break-in last night." Mr. Toland, Jr. drew the attention of the crowd to the door in question with an exaggerated nod of his head. The door was not easy to miss. Its shattered pane of glass had been replaced by cardboard and duct tape. "We are still open for business, and you are free to enter, but you must know that there are certain items that are no longer in stock. You will not find them here and you will not be permitted to hound my store clerk Miss Choate about it. She has far too much to do, since all of my other clerks cannot make it in to work due to advanced age."

A woman raised her hand. "Please give us that list of unavailable items if you would."

"Yes. I have the list right here." Mr. Toland, Jr. pulled a small piece of paper from his shirt pocket. He took a pair of eyeglasses out of a different pocket and put them on. He cleared his throat. "Oatmeal, Cream-of-Wheat, and other soft cereals."

A collective gasp went up from the crowd.

"All Jell-O products. All gelatins of every kind. All custards and box puddings."

"Even Tapioca?" asked a man in the back.

"Yes. Tapioca and every other kind of box pudding. Also Postum. And Malt-o-Meal. That goes under the heading of soft cereals. Let me see—oh, and all soft fruit that can be easily gummed."

Another gasp. A different woman raised her hand.

"Yes, Miss Edwards?"

"But that leaves nothing for my mother to eat. She is now 104 and has no teeth!"

"I am sorry Miss Edwards, but it is out of my hands."

"When will you get in more soft foods from the warehouse?"

"There are no more soft foods in the warehouse. They have also been taken, and no one knows when they will be replaced with a new shipment."

Now Davy Rockwell raised his hand. "Excuse me, Mr. Toland, but what about the other stores around town? Do you know if they have soft foods in stock—foods that are easy on the digestion and if necessary may be gummed rather than chewed?"

"I have spoken with the managers and owners of the other food markets in town—or, rather, I have spoken with their sons and daughters who are now running their fathers' stores, and I am told that each of those stores was also robbed last night. As I understand it, there is no more soft food available for purchase anywhere in the town of Pitcherville."

Rodney and Wayne turned to each other and exchanged astonished looks. "What about Aunt Mildred? What will she eat?" said Wayne in a low voice.

"And the Professor too? And everyone else who will now require a soft and mushy diet?"

The two boys shook their heads worriedly. It was a sad state of affairs for a town without blenders.

(Pitcherville had no blenders in the year 1956. Craft Appliances had begun to sell them right after they came out in the 1930s, but then an accident involving an overly-curious, careless customer whose name is not important to this story—but who could easily be identified by a deficiency in the number of fingers on his right hand—motivated Mr. Craft to send all of his blenders back to their manufacturers and to order no more for the sake of other customer fingers.)

Davy Rockwell raised his hand again. "Can this really be true? Can it really be true that there is no soft food available for purchase anywhere in the town of Pitcherville?"

"Of course not! That is ridiculous!" Davy's question was answered by a tall man, whom Rodney and Wayne could not quite see at that moment except for the back of his head, which had a prominent bald spot in the middle of it. "I know where there is plenty of food matching that description."

"Let him through!" said a man.

"Yes, let him speak!" shouted a different man. "He knows where soft food can be had."

The crowd parted so that the tall man and a shorter man standing beside him could move to the front. Mr. Toland, Jr. stepped down from his crate and offered it to the tall man.

"Get a load of *that*!" said Wayne under his breath. "It's Jackie. And lookit! Lonnie's right with him!"

"I'll bet those two had something to do with all the robberies last night," said Rodney.

"Hello, my good friends and neighbors," said Jackie, speaking in a loud and overly-formal speech-giving voice. Maybe you don't recognize me and my business partner here. So allow us to introduce ourselves. I am Jackie Stovall—yes, your ol' friend Jackie Stovall. And this is Lonnie Rowe."

"You mean the same Jackie Stovall and Lonnie Rowe who turned over my Fluffy's doghouse?" shouted Sharon, bristling.

"The same Jackie and Lonnie who let all the air out of my father's tires?" yelled Davy.

"N'est pas? N'est pas?" asked Virgil.

Jackie lowered his outstretched palms to silence the murmurs of the small crowd of people glowering in front of him. "No, no, my friends, that was the *old* Jackie and Lonnie. Standing before you here today are the *new* Jackie and Lonnie. We have turned over a brand new leaf. For we are in the midst of a terrible crisis, ladies and gentlemen, and we must come together as one community." Jackie joined all of his fingers together to show how a town of people could come together, provided that they all looked like fingers. "Someone, and we do not know who, has stolen all of the soft food that was for sale in the town of Pitcherville. A tragedy! An offense against nature! But I ask all of you on this dark day: will we stand idly by and allow the oldest of our citizens to starve? No, we most certainly will not!"

A woman started to clap her hands in support of what Jackie had just said but was so strongly frowned upon by the people standing around her that she immediately stopped. You see, most of the people standing around the woman had been victims of Jackie and Lonnie's pranks and other acts of youthful vandalism, and were not yet convinced that the two had actually turned over a brand new leaf.

"So here is what Lonnie and I will do. Because we predicted that this thing might happen and prepared for it—because we had—had—now, what is the word?

"Head lice?" snickered someone in the crowd.

"No," said Jackie, glowering at the person.

"Foresight?" offered someone else.

"Yes, foresight. Because we had the foresight, Lonnie and me, to scrape together as much money as we could to spend the last several months buying up a large quantity of soft food—food which is now sitting safe and sound in a secret location—because we have done this, ladies and gentlemen, we can now stand before you and reach out a helping hand." Jackie reached out his hand to show how easy it was to do such a thing. "We have searched our souls, friends and neighbors, and decided that we have no right to keep that soft food to ourselves. No sir, we do not. So we will be rationing it out to all of those in need."

"How much do you plan to take us for?" called out the man who had said "head lice."

"Take you for?" Jackie seemed greatly offended by the question. He placed his hand on his chest to emphasize how offended and hurt and generally taken aback he was by such rudeness. "Perhaps you won't believe me, but I don't intend to charge you a single penny. Why? I will tell you why. Because we will use the barter system. I will give you, say a cup of Cream-of-Wheat, in exchange for something that you give *me*. Now, for example, I have made a bargain with my very own father, the Mayor. He has no teeth. He *had* teeth—false teeth, that is—but someone, regrettably, has stolen them from him." Jackie shook his head dolefully over how such a terrible thing could happen.

"It is also regrettable that my father is now confined to his bed and can no longer carry out his duties as mayor. Nor is there anything in the house that he and my poor mother can eat. It is a most difficult situation however you look at it.

"Now, friends and neighbors, I will show all of you how this works: I will take my poor, bedridden and toothless father a cup of Malt-o-Meal. In exchange for this, he will make *me*, his son, the new mayor of the town of Pitcherville."

There rose up another collective gasp from the crowd. One man shouted, "Outrage!"

"Who said that?" asked Jackie, craning his head to look around. "Whoever said that will not be doing business with me. No soft cereal, no custard, not even a squishy over-ripe plum! Now, once I have gotten myself settled into the mayor's office at City Hall, you may all begin to form a line outside my door. I will open my door promptly at eight o'clock tomorrow morning to see the first people in the line. My deputy, Mr. Rowe, will dispense the foodstuffs after we have come to our individual agreements. I assure you all that no one will go hungry in this town, not while I am the mayor! Good day, my good friends and neighbors and bon—bon—what is the word?"

"Voyage?" asked a woman in the crowd.

"No, no. The other word. The food word."

"Appetit," offered Virgil confidently.

"Yes, bon appetit to you all."

With that, Jackie stepped down from the speaking crate and departed, along with his newly appointed deputy Lonnie.

A stunned silence followed, and then a soft, whispered exchange or two, and in no time at all a big noisy, earnest and fearful buzz.

"I do not want my mother to starve in her bed!" said one woman. "I'll give the man anything he asks for."

"What else *can* we do?" said her companion.

"He certainly has us over a barrel," said Davy Rockwell, shaking his head despondently. "I have to feed all of my grandparents. I have a grandfather who must now be nearly 130 years old! He wasn't eating solid food even before all of this happened. I'm going over to the mayor's office right now. I want to be first in line when he opens his door tomorrow. Goodbye, boys. It was good to see you again."

Davy hurried off. There were others who, probably thinking the same thing, hurried off in the very same direction.

CHAPTER ELEVEN

In which Officer Wall delivers bad news and Rodney and Wayne learn what is in their father's secret cellar

When Rodney and Wayne explained the situation to the Professor, the old man said, "That's extortion! It's monstrous! That bully-boy intends to be an outright dictator!"

"What can we do about it, Professor?" asked Rodney. "You and Aunt Mildred will have to eat."

"You must be resourceful, boys. Doesn't your great aunt do a little canning? What has she put up from last year?"

"Some green beans and squash."

"Nothing soft and squishy and not too acidic or too seedy? Seeds are never good for the tracts of old people."

"We'll find out," said Rodney. "Also, there is still a little oatmeal in her cupboard. And we noticed a box of pudding mix in your pantry."

"Is it Tapioca? I love Tapioca."

"I don't remember."

"Well, there is enough food around—if we do a thorough job of scrounging—to feed your great aunt and me for the next two days—perhaps even three or four if we each take small bites. And in the meantime, we must work as hard as we are able to finish the new Age Altertron. Now go down and complete your inventory and then, if there is time left, I would not mind some hot pudding."

Rodney and Wayne completed their inventory and cooked some pudding and then worked through the night on the first phase of construction for the new machine. The Professor sat in an arm chair not too far from the work area, wrapped in a blanket to keep away the chill, consulting his calculations and his diagrams and shouting out instructions in his increasingly raspy voice: "Tighten that bolt! Excellent! The red wire and now the green wire! Now why is there no charge in that auxiliary battery? I wonder what has happened to the multi-volt charger? Can you find the thermionic triode pentode? What have I done with it? Think, Russell, think! And why have I reversed the electrostatic charge? Would someone please tell me that? Ah, there is our oddleg caliper. Gizmo had been sleeping on it!"

The Professor also took time to explain the mechanics and physics of the Age Altertron II so that Rodney and Wayne would have a better understanding of what they were doing. "When we age, boys, the cells in our bodies decay and die. Conversely, if a man were to grow incrementally younger, there would be a rebirth of cellular tissue within his body. Now this is what the Age Altertron does: depending on whether you wish it to age a man or give him sudden youth, the machine sends signals throughout a prescribed area—in our case, the town of Pitcherville—that either destroy the components of human cellular growth or stimulate them. The pulse of the signal is multiplied exponentially to create a nearly instantaneous result. Now did you understand any of that?"

"A little," said Wayne sheepishly.

By morning the boys were exhausted but proud of all they had accomplished. The Professor was equally proud of his two apprentices and how hard they had worked. "I was afraid that we would be unable to recover from the damage that I did last night," the boys' scientific mentor said with a crusty voice, "but this is a most admirable start. I wish that there were some way I could repay you two for all the good work you are doing."

"You've repaid us enough with everything you've done for this town over the last year, Professor," said Rodney.

Becky, who had come by to bring egg-and-olive sandwiches to Rodney and Wayne, nodded in agreement.

"But there is nothing that I can do, specifically, for you kids?"

"Well, now that you mention it," said Wayne, grinning mischievously, "you could let me take your Nash out for a spin."

"What is that, Wayne? I didn't hear you."

Wayne was about to repeat his request with more volume when he was interrupted by a knock at the door. Becky jumped up to answer it. "Hello, Officer Wall. Won't you come in?"

Officer Wall, who now had the wrinkled face of a man in his

eighties, hobbled into the laboratory using a cane. He was no longer wearing his policeman's uniform. "Good morning, Professor. Good morning, Rodney, Wayne, Becky."

"Are we being too loud?" asked Wayne.

"No, no. You are well within the noise limit. I have come to tell you something I believe you should know."

"Please sit down, Officer," said Rodney. Together he and Wayne helped the slow-moving officer down onto a bench.

"Ah. That feels good. It is a long walk from City Hall. I no longer have my patrol car, you see."

"Why is that?" asked Wayne.

"It doesn't belong to me anymore. I have been fired—no, I believe that the proper word is 'retired.' I have been purposefully 'retired' from the police force."

"But why?"

"Look at me. I can hardly walk. Let alone breathe. My asthma is much worse. It is for the best. I was at the new mayor's office this morning. There was a very long line. People are worried and depressed. This calamity is taking a terrible toll on the oldest citizens of this town and on everyone who loves them. But the ones waiting in line took some pity on me and let me go ahead. When I stand for too long, my knee joints seize up and then I walk around as if I am walking on stilts."

"So what did you need to see the Mayor about?"

"There has been no mention of whether I am entitled to a pension. My wife and I have no income now. I needed to find out if there will be a little money for us to live on."

"And what did the Mayor say?"

"That I had to discuss it with his new police chief."

"Who is the new police chief?" asked the Professor. He held a cup of warm beef broth in both hands. Becky had just brewed it for him. It was not as fine a meal as oatmeal and mashed bananas, but it did keep the hunger pangs away for a while at least.

"It's Lonnie. Lonnie Rowe, the boy my partner and I arrested for helping to incite the City Park baby carriage riot. Jackie, now *Mayor* Stovall, eluded us. But we got Lonnie and kept him in jail for a whole day. He is now the new police chief. I'm sure that he will take vengeance on me and I will see no pension. But that is neither here nor there. Oh look, there's your little terrier, Professor. Where are his earmuffs?"

"He only wears them when there are loud noises to contend with. Please, go on."

"Yes. Well, as you can see, it takes me a little while to get from Point A to Point B. It took me an extra minute or two to leave the Mayor's office after our chat. During that time I overheard a conversation between the Mayor and his new police chief that he probably didn't think I could hear. But I can actually still hear quite well. Perhaps it comes from all those years of listening closely for potential noise violations."

"What did you overhear, Officer Wall?" asked Becky.

"The Mayor was asking the police chief to send some of his men—the younger men, that is, those who have just joined the force—not any of the old codgers like myself who are now too rusty to do our jobs—to send them here to this house, with an order to destroy all the equipment in this lab. All the tools, all of your notebooks, everything. He wants to shut your laboratory down, Professor Johnson."

"Upon what grounds!" cried the Professor. So unsettling was

this report from the former police officer that Professor Johnson started to rise up from his chair, knotting himself in his blanket and sloshing his broth all about.

"Upon the grounds that your laboratory poses a danger to the town of Pitcherville. He said that he heard there was a fire here last night. Now, I don't know if there was one or not…"

"There was," admitted Rodney solemnly.

"And he says he cannot trust that there will not be other fires with a doddering old fool at work here."

The Professor grimaced when Officer Wall said "doddering old fool." It was a look of anger and hurt.

Officer Wall continued: "And with all the chemicals and potentially explosive materials in this laboratory no one could be sure that the next fire wouldn't be far worse than the last, or could even result in the whole neighborhood being blown to smithereens! And that is all of the conversation I heard, for by then I had reached the door. But that was plenty to hear, don't you think?"

"Oh it was more than enough, Officer Wall, and I appreciate your telling us." The Professor settled himself back into his chair. "Do you children see what our new mayor is doing?"

Rodney nodded. "Jackie must know that we are working on a new Age Altertron. And he must know that once we finish it and all of us have been returned to our true ages, he won't be able to hold on to his power over this town any more—that his days of being a dictator will be over. Then he and Lonnie will have to go back to being the two juvenile delinquent nobodies they have always been!"

"Well put, Rodney," said the Professor. "So where shall we move all of this equipment to continue our work on the machine in secret?"

"How about your sub-basement?" suggested Wayne.

"And who was it who told us about the Professor's sub-basement, Wayne?" asked Rodney, arching an eyebrow at his brother.

"Well—let me—*oh*. It was Jackie. But is it true, Professor?"

"It is true. I am trying to think of how Jackie would come to know about my several basements, though."

"Well, Professor," said Officer Wall, "he and Lonnie have always made it their habit to sneak into places where they could hide from my fellow officers and me."

"And you *do* like to leave you laboratory door unlocked, Professor," added Wayne.

"Well, now that the truth is out, Wayne, I will admit that I not only have a basement and a sub-basement but even a cellar and a sub-cellar below those."

"Why so many underground rooms, Professor?" asked Wayne.

"I will tell you some day, but not today. Suffice it to say, Jackie and Lonnie know of the basements, so we will have to think of some other place to move our lab. Let us put our heads together, kids; where is the last place that those two thugs would think of looking for my Age Altertron?"

"Well," said Rodney, "I know of a cellar that few people know about—a cellar that even I have never seen."

"Where is it?"

"Beneath my very own house."

"What is Rodney talking about, Wayne?" asked Becky. "You two never told me there was a cellar under your house."

Wayne nodded. "It's a secret cellar. It was built over a hundred years ago, at the time that the house was built."

"The cellar was a place for slaves to hide," explained Rodney. "Slaves who were escaping from their Confederate masters before the outbreak of the Civil War. You see, our father's house was once a stop on the Underground Railroad."

The Professor whistled his surprise. "And in this case the word 'underground' may be applied quite literally! I had no idea, Rodney. And I happen to know a great deal about the history of this town."

"Well that was the idea—that no one should know about it, except the people who were *supposed* to know about it, the people who wanted to help the runaway slaves."

"But why have you two never seen it?" asked Becky. "What is down there now?"

Rodney lowered his voice dramatically, as if to add a note of mystery to his story. "Well, that is the second half of the tale. My father started building something down there. Something secret. He began building it when Wayne and I were very small. He said that someday he would show it to us. In fact, he said that he hoped to be able to show it to us when we turned seventeen."

The Professor looked puzzled. "Why seventeen, Rodney? Is there some significance to that age that is momentarily escaping me?"

Wayne answered for his brother: "There is no significance about our being seventeen, Professor. What is significant is the year that he wanted to show it to us: 1960."

"1960. How curious. I cannot think why that year should hold such meaning for your father. Can *you*, Officer Wall?"

"I didn't know your father very well so I couldn't say. The year holds no special meaning for *me*, although 1960 will be the year I turn ninety if your machine doesn't return us all to our real ages."

"We must go talk to Aunt Mildred, Rodney," said Wayne. "She knows about the cellar. And she also knows what's down there.

Maybe she'll let us work on the machine there if what our father has left there can be set aside. It can't be any more important than what we are doing to save this town. I'm sure that Dad would agree."

The Professor nodded. "Wayne, you make a very good case."

"An astute case?" asked Wayne, hopefully.

"Most astute, my boy. Now you and Rodney go speak to your aunt. I'll remain and nap so that I will be fresh to continue work on my calculations. We cannot afford for me to make another mistake. I must have seven naps a day, you see, and by my latest estimation, I am two behind."

Rodney and Wayne found their Aunt Mildred awake. She was lying in bed listening to her radio. In the stronger light, Aunt Mildred looked very different from her earlier, younger self. She was tiny and frail with a face that wrapped itself so tightly about her skull that she appeared almost skeletal. Save only a few patches of fine, wispy hair, she had no hair at all. "Are you listening to your favorite soap opera, Aunt Mildred?" asked Wayne.

"I was for a while. You may wish to know that poor Delores finally got her memory back. But then a brick fell on her head and the amnesia returned. Just as the program was switching to a commercial for Plash Detergent—you know the one I like with those sweet little girls who sing: 'Plash, Plash, won't give you a rash!'—well, all of the sudden there he is—the new mayor, giving a speech! Can you believe it? That hooligan interrupting *Helen Grant, Backstage Nurse* for no good reason at all!"

"Well, he had to have *some* reason," said Rodney.

"Yes," said Wayne. "What did the hooligan have to say?"

"Let me see if I remember. Something about plans to put every-one over the age of one hundred into a special city nursing home. But he wasn't very clear: did he mean people who were over the age of one hundred *before* all this happened, or after? If he means after, why, that's over one third of all the people in this town!"

"I think that's exactly what he means, Aunt Mildred," said Rodney.

"Well, dear me. I don't want to go to a city nursing home. There won't be nearly enough beds and we'll probably all have to share. And what if I get someone in my bed who doesn't like cinnamon and won't let me put my cinnamon sachet under my pillow every night?"

Rodney looked at Wayne. Things were about to get even worse than they already were. Jackie was going to get rid of all the old people, pure and simple! He was going to place them all into a big industrial-sized nursing home and lock all the doors and put the matter of how best to care for all the old people totally out of mind.

Wayne took his great aunt's hand, and laid it tenderly into the palm of his own hand. "Rodney and I have a favor to ask of you, Aunt Mildred. It's something that the Professor wants too."

Aunt Mildred's face suddenly lit up. "The Professor wants me to do something for him? What is it? You know I would do anything for that lovely man."

"We have to hide the Professor's laboratory. Otherwise the police are going to come and destroy it. Then we won't be able to finish the new Age Altertron.

"Oh dear. Where are you thinking about hiding it?"

"In Dad's cellar."

"You mean the one downstairs? You mean the one underneath this house?"

Wayne and Rodney both nodded. "The Underground Railroad station," said Rodney.

"But his *project* is down there—the project he was working on for almost a dozen years. He started it shortly after you were born. It helped him to ease the pain of missing your mother so much."

"Is it finished?" asked Rodney.

"Well, I don't know if he's finished it or not. I suppose he hasn't. It wasn't scheduled to be completed, as you know, until 1960."

"What is so special about 1960?"

"I promised him that I wouldn't spoil his surprise and tell you anything else about it." Aunt Mildred thought for a moment, and then she added: "And he would be most upset should you see it before he wanted you to."

Rodney swallowed hard. "Aunt Mildred. This is probably the only cellar in Pitcherville that Jackie and Lonnie don't know about. Dad would understand. I'm sure of it. Besides, what if the project he was working on had something to do with his disappearance? Isn't it important for us to go down there for *that* reason alone? So you have to give us the key that unlocks that secret door inside the broom closet. We really need you to do this. The *Professor* really needs it too. Our father may never be coming back. So it may end up making no difference at all whether he would be disappointed that we saw his surprise before he wanted us to see it. But Wayne and I don't want to lose you. And we don't want to lose the Professor. That's what's important right now."

"You really think Dad's not coming back, Rodney?" asked Wayne.

"There is that chance—the chance we may never see him again."

"Gee, Rodney. I always try not to think about that."

"I know. I do too. But I've also known that there would come some day when we'd have to face that possibility. Maybe that day is today, Wayne."

Wayne wiped the moistness in his eyes with the back of his hand.

"Oh dear," was all that Aunt Mildred could say. Then she grew quiet as she studied a pattern on her bedroom wallpaper. Tears began to form in her own eyes. She turned back to her great-nephews and said, "The official name for The World of Tomorrow exhibit inside the big Perisphere at the World's Fair was 'Democracity.' It was a diorama that imagined what the world could look like in the future—a perfect world where there was peace and freedom, and no one went to bed hungry. A place where everything ran smoothly and efficiently. You stood upon a walkway and looked down at the city from the sky. I think it was the largest diorama ever made—tiny cars and miniature buildings, little in size but quite large if one were to actually build them to full scale.

"Well, your father started to build his own Democracity diorama right there on the floor of his secret cellar, fashioning every little tree, every house, every tiny car with his own hands. He wanted to have it finished by the year 1960 for a reason. You see, that is the exact year that was depicted in the diorama at the World's Fair. It was to be a city of the future—what could the world be like in that far-off year? Every night he would go down there to work on it after he had put you boys to bed. It was quite a labor of love."

"I wish that you had let us see it right after he left," said Wayne sullenly. "Maybe it wasn't such a good idea to make us wait nearly a whole year."

"Well, considering the circumstances in which we now find ourselves I'm almost positive that your father would now agree to using it for the Professor's new laboratory. So take the key from that top drawer of my dresser and unlock the padlock and go down to your father's secret cellar and tuck his city away as carefully as you can. I have not seen it in over a year, but I remember that he was making fine progress with it. Take care not to crush a single tree or wrinkle a single bright-green lawn."

"We will, Aunt Mildred," said Rodney and Wayne in perfect unison.

And so down the two boys went into their father's secret cellar to see the product of twelve years of painstaking, meticulous work. There was no light switch at the top of the stairs but there was a pull cord that hung two or three steps down. Wayne gave it a yank as each boy held his breath, not even imagining how strange and wonderful their father's own version of Democracity would look to their eager eyes.

Unfortunately, all that lay before them was a bare floor. There was nothing there. Democracity II, or "The World of Tomorrow Revisited," as Mitch McCall had hoped to call his project, had disappeared along with its maker.

CHAPTER TWELVE

In which things go very well for several days until the day
on which things don't go very well at all

The laboratory was quickly and safely installed within the McCall cellar—every diode and every triode, every notebook and tiniest scrap of scribbled paper, every caliper and slide rule, every screwdriver and wrench and pair of needle-nose pliers. This was all accomplished that very night under the helpful cover of darkness and by use of one of Mr. Craft's appliance delivery vans.

Rodney and Wayne and the Professor had sought to keep the circle of those who knew the location of the new laboratory to a very small number of trusted individuals: Mr. Craft, of course, and his daughter Becky, and Petey Ragsdale and Grover Ferrell, and Officer Wall and Aunt Mildred. There were others such as Mrs. Ferrell and Mr. and Mrs. Ragsdale who knew some things about the laboratory's relocation but didn't know everything, and then there was a large group of people, including Mayor Stovall and Police Chief Lonnie Rowe, who knew absolutely nothing at all. And that was the way that Rodney and Wayne and the Professor liked it.

The next morning, the Professor and his two apprentices set up their new laboratory. The morning after that they resumed work on Age Altertron II. Comings and goings at the McCall house were kept to a minimum to reduce suspicion. The sofa in Mr. McCall's bear cave was turned into a bed for the Professor. Places were made on the floor for Gizmo and Tesla (at opposite ends of the room). The Professor was not concerned by the small size of the room so long as its occupancy did not exceed six at any one time. All the nights he stayed there he never once found it necessary to put his head out of the window and suck in air.

For her part, Aunt Mildred was so delighted to have the Professor for a live-in guest that she found the strength to leave her bed and even to prepare a light snack or two for him in the kitchen. In return for her hospitality Professor Johnson spent a little time instructing Rodney and Wayne in the invention of a "Rotary Liquidizer," which worked the same way as a blender. The Professor's Liquidizer allowed the two oldest members of the household to eat more foods than they had previously been able to eat.

When she heard about the Professor's new invention, Becky, being a considerate girl, decided to come over to the McCall home each night to liquefy food for the benefit of the hungriest of her older neighbors—and especially those who had run out of things to barter with the Mayor. Then, when she was finished at that late hour when the Professor could no longer keep his eyes open, either Rodney or Wayne, or both of the boys together, would walk her home.

During these walks Becky would open her heart and talk about how much she had wanted to be a pediatrician, and how much she loved little children, and how much she wanted at least seven children of her own, and how sad it would be if she lost her youth forever. Rodney and Wayne would become silent and tongue-tied in the face of her deep, empty longing. The twins would feel affection for her but not know quite how to show it, since she was a girl and since girls had to be handled in a different way than other people.

After they had delivered Becky to her door, the boys would continue on to the Professor's house to see if the police had come. For several nights there was no evidence that they had. The halves of playing cards that Rodney and Wayne had discreetly placed between each of the outside doors and their jambs were always in the very same spots in which they had been left. This was an indication to the boys that no one had entered the house in their absence.

In fact, it wasn't even necessary for Rodney and Wayne to enter the house themselves, since they could see from the outside that it remained secure.

Until, that is, the fifth night…the night that would bring this story to its close.

Much had happened during the day that led up to that important night: the Professor had pronounced the new Age Altertron nearly finished. All that was required was a couple more hours of work and then the machine would be ready for testing. If the tests went well the next day, Age Altertron II could be switched on the very next night at midnight, the time at which both calamities and their corrections took place.

Most people would be safe in their beds and would not find themselves startled or liable to do injury to themselves during that transformational moment in which the correction took place. The unfortunate circumstances surrounding the loss of the first Altertron is a good example of the bad that can happen when one is up and about at that moment. Perhaps this was the reason that the unknown force chose to inflict its calamities upon the town so late at night.

Or not. (The unknown force had not otherwise demonstrated much concern for the health and well-being of the citizens of Pitcherville.)

The day had been busy and productive, and hopes ran high among the Professor's small circle of helpers that this newest calamity would soon be a memory.

Hopes and spirits remained high, in fact, right up to 2:17 p.m., when a ringing doorbell set off a chain of events that would upend every effort to save the town of Pitcherville from this latest calamity *and* from those who would use it to their own sinister advantage.

Rodney and Wayne and the Professor did not hear the doorbell because of the noise being made by Wayne's pneumatic hypersonic-hammering and Rodney's dyna-turbonic drilling. And, besides, the cellar was a very tightly sealed room with no windows and its only door hidden in a broom closet. It was hard for them to hear *anything* down there.

The only person who did hear the ring was Aunt Mildred. She was upstairs in her bed listening to her radio program. Like most of the very old residents of Pitcherville, Aunt Mildred had grown weaker over the last few days, as if her body were giving up in its struggle to keep its occupant alive until the calamity could be reversed. A great number of older Pitchervillians, in fact, were now drawing very close to their final hours, their super-aged bodies ready for permanent and eternal retirement.

Aunt Mildred could not have reached the door in any reasonable amount of time. So she lay there in her upstairs bedroom and wondered who the visitor was. If his reason for coming was important, he would, no doubt, come back, and if it wasn't he wouldn't.

Or there was a third thing that could happen. The visitor could break the door down. Which he proceeded to do with the help of two police officers.

Such activity tends to make a fairly loud noise *and* a reverberation in all the walls of a house, and so down in the cellar Wayne had every reason to ask, "Hey! Did either of you feel that?"

"Yes I did," replied the Professor. "It is probably the transducer oscillating too low. Take it up to 7.8."

Upstairs, Aunt Mildred not only felt the vibrations of her front door being knocked down, she also *heard* it, and quickly grew frightened. She sat up in bed and pulled the covers up to her chin (in that way frightened people in beds often do, believing that the sheets and blankets will serve as a good shield against bedroom intruders).

"Miss McCall! Miss McCall!" came a man's voice from downstairs.

Aunt Mildred didn't know if it would be wise to keep silent or to let the home invaders know where she was. Thinking they would find her eventually, she saved them a little trouble and directed them to her bedroom. "I'm up here! But please bear in mind that I am not inviting you up here to hurt me!"

A couple of moments later, three men entered the room: Police Chief Lonnie Rowe and two of his officers. There was also a woman with them, Miss Carter, who had been hired to assist the police department in a special operation that had begun that day. You see, it was Miss Carter's job to help the women centenarians (that is, those women who had reached the age of one hundred or older) gather up their things so that they could be transported to the brand new city nursing home.

"The new nursing home is finished already?" asked Aunt Mildred after Miss Carter had explained everything to her.

"Yes. The Mayor wanted it completed as soon as possible. It really is nothing more than our town high school gymnasium fitted with cots and footlockers. I am sorry to report that we haven't enough cots for all of you so a few will have to sleep on pallets on the floor."

"But I do not wish to go, Lucinda. Why do I have to go?"

"It is the law."

"Why is it the law? What is wrong with my staying in my own home? I have people to look after me."

"But that is the problem. Everyone is wasting too much time taking care of the old ones and cannot do the jobs that must be done in our town. We have had no milk deliveries or egg deliveries for three days. The barbershops and beauty parlors are all closed. And there is no one at the filling stations to pump our gas and check under our hoods. My own grandmother, to give you an example, requires constant care. Now all of you will receive care together in one large group. It is very economical this way. Now gather up your things. You are permitted a small piece of luggage and one shopping bag."

As Miss Carter was helping Aunt Mildred up from the bed, Lonnie asked, "Where are your nephews? Are they not here?"

"No, they are with the Professor." Aunt Mildred didn't mean to say that. It just slipped out.

"And where *is* the Professor? We've been looking for him for several days. We know he isn't at his house anymore. Do you know where he's gone?"

Aunt Mildred shook her head.

"Well, when you see one of your nephews or the Professor, you should mention that the playing-card-in-the-door trick hasn't worked since 1932. We've been visiting his house every day this week. We've been all over it, looking for clues to where he could have taken his laboratory. We've found no clues yet but we did find something that might be of interest to the Professor. We're surprised that he hasn't missed it yet."

"What is it?"

"I am not at liberty to tell you."

"May I leave a note for Rodney and Wayne to tell them where I've gone?" asked Aunt Mildred, as she put one of her several tubs of night cream into her one allowable shopping bag.

The new police chief nodded. "You may also add the fact that there is now a warrant for your nephews' arrest."

"For doing what?"

"For obstructing the law by helping Professor Johnson move his laboratory to a secret location. And as of this afternoon for harboring a fugitive."

"What fugitive?"

Police Chief Rowe laughed. "Well, Professor Johnson, of course. As of this afternoon he is officially a fugitive from the city nursing home. Mayor Stovall is not a man to be taken lightly, lady."

Downstairs in the cellar, Wayne was about to put the cover housing over the Age Altertron II, which, when properly contained, looked like a large console record player with the doors shut. There was a bank of knobs and buttons inset into its front, and a number of antennas of various lengths sprouting from the top and from both sides. "Do we need to do another inspection, Professor, or is everything okay?"

"It is fine as far as I can tell," answered the Professor, "and ready for testing to begin first thing in the morning. What is it, Rodney? Is something wrong?"

Rodney chewed upon his lower lip for a moment. He was thinking. "Well, I see the primary beam deflector and there is the secondary beam deflector, but there is no tertiary beam deflector. Your diagram shows that it should be right behind the capacitor."

"My boy, you're exactly right. Did we not install it?"

Wayne shook his head. "It isn't there."

"Could we actually have left it behind?" The Professor stroked his several-day-old whiskers (which were still not much more than stubble, since whiskers do not grow very fast on the faces of 117-year-old men). "Yet the room was totally empty when we left—not a paper clip, not even the smallest triode prong."

The Professor thought for a moment, pacing in his chair by moving his feet back and forth. Then it hit him. In that next moment he knew: "Because the tertiary beam deflector wasn't *in* the laboratory. I had taken it from the rubble of my first ruined machine and put it into the pocket of my lab coat."

"Why would you want to do *that*, Professor?" asked Wayne.

"Oh, I intended to spend the rest of the night scavenging all of the parts that I could use again, but exhaustion overtook me in just the short time it took to deposit the deflector. I suspect it is still in my coat pocket, which I am certain is still hanging in my bedroom closet."

"I'll go and get it," volunteered Wayne.

"Let me go with you, Wayne," said Rodney. "One of us should serve as look-out for the other in case the police show up."

"Be careful, boys," said the Professor, easing back into his chair.

Rodney and Wayne climbed the cellar stairs, opened the door that put them into the hallway broom closet and then the second door that opened onto the hallway itself. "Aunt Mildred!" Wayne called up the stairs. "We have to go to the Professor's. We'll be back soon."

No answer.

"Aunt Mildred! Are you sleeping?"

"Now Wayne, what did I tell you about asking questions that can only be answered one way?"

"Well, 'No, I'm not sleeping' was the answer I was looking for."

Not hearing that answer, the boys climbed the stairs to look in on their unresponsive great aunt. The room was empty. Aunt Mildred was gone. But her radio was still on. The new mayor of Pitcherville was giving another of his speeches. He was saying, "… know that this is for everyone's good. Our oldest citizens will be well cared for and there is no cause for concern. You may visit your loved ones on alternate Sundays from 2:15 until 2:30 in the afternoon. Anyone attempting to circumvent this law will be subject to immediate arrest and prosecution."

"They have taken Aunt Mildred," said Rodney.

"Along with all the other old people, I'll bet. All of them, except for Professor Johnson. What are we going to do, Rodney?"

"Get the tertiary beam deflector from his coat pocket and hurry back here as quickly as we can. I am sure that once we tell the Professor what is happening, he will not want to wait until tomorrow night to activate the new Age Altertron. We can run our tests tonight and be ready to flip the switch by midnight."

Wayne nodded. He noticed a sealed envelope at the foot of the bed. "What's this?"

He picked it up. Though the handwriting on the outside was crabbed and hard to read, it looked as if it were addressed to Rodney and him.

Wayne tore open the envelope and pulled out the letter that was inside. He read it aloud to his brother:

> My dear Rodney and Wayne:
> No doubt you realize by now what has happened to me.
> I will miss you, dear boys. Please take good care of yourselves. Eat your vegetables. If you sprinkle some cinnamon on them they will taste even better.
> By the way, there is a warrant out for your arrest, so you might want to go back to you-know-where and stay there!
> Love,
> Aunt Mildred

"We can't go to the Professor's house now," said Rodney. "If Lonnie isn't waiting for us just outside, he's probably lying in wait somewhere along the way, ready to ambush and arrest us."

"Then we should go back down to the cellar like Aunt Mildred says."

"And then what, Wayne? Sit around and do nothing without the tertiary beam deflector?"

"Maybe the Professor can tell us how to make a new deflector."

"And how long will *that* take when we've never worked with such small components before?

Wayne shrugged. Rodney sat down on the bed. He took the letter from his brother's hand and turned it over in his own hand, thinking of his great aunt.

"Smell the letter," said Wayne.

Rodney took a whiff of Aunt Mildred's scented letter.

Cinnamon, to remember her by.

CHAPTER THIRTEEN

*In which Wayne finally gets to drive the Professor's car
and you the reader finally
get to the end of
this book*

Petey and Grover would be the decoys. They would come out of the McCall house looking as much like Rodney and Wayne as they were able (considering that Petey was shorter and Grover was wider). They would wear fedora hats with the brims tilted down and hiding their faces in shadow and would mount Rodney and Wayne's bikes and then ride slowly to the Professor's house by the street route. The boys hoped somebody would be watching the McCall house and would take the bait. Then Rodney and Wayne could slip out and go the opposite way on foot, taking a circuitous route that wound through several backyards, and down a drainage ditch and through City Park. If they were quick enough and their friends Petey and Grover slow enough Rodney and Wayne would beat their friends to the Professor's house and would be in and out, deflector in hand, before anyone else arrived. This was the plan.

And the plan worked. At least the first part.

An unmarked car, which had been parked a block from the McCall home, now began to shadow Petey and Grover as they steered their bikes slowly down the street, both boys wobbling a little because their older heavier bodies sat differently upon the light Schwinn cruisers. Rodney and Wayne made very good time with their foot route, which required some fence scaling and some ditch crossing that taxed their new-old muscles and tired their new-old lungs.

As planned, the twins arrived first at the Professor's house and quickly stole through the back gate. They entered the house through the back door to what had earlier been the Professor's laboratory. The old house was dark, but they did not dare turn on any of the lights.

Stumbling a little in the darkness Rodney and Wayne made their way to the stairs and then up to the Professor's bedroom. While Rodney stood just outside the closet, Wayne stepped inside and closed the door so that he could turn on the flashlight he had brought, and no one would see its light from outside the house. "Gee, there sure are a lot of lab coats in here!" remarked Wayne in a muffled voice from inside the closet.

"Then you'll have to look through all the pockets," said Rodney to the closet door. "The deflector shouldn't be hard to find. It's about four inches high and two inches around. Be careful not to prick yourself on the connectors."

After a moment, Wayne said, "I can't find it. There's nothing in any of these pockets but a couple of peanuts and a piece of paper."

"Pull out the piece of paper."

"Can I have the peanuts too, Rodney? I'm kind of hungry."

"The paper, Wayne. What's on the paper?"

"It's probably nothing. Wait. It's something."

"What does it say, Wayne?"

"It's a letter to *us*!"

"Is it from the Professor?"

"No."

"Who else would put a letter to us into the Professor's lab coat pocket?"

"Who do you think, Rodney?" Wayne read the note aloud to his brother:

Hi Monkeys,

Guess what used to be in this pocket? Something important, I'll bet. And how do I know this? Because of how carefully the Professor cleaned it before he put it in here. And how do I know this? Because I was watching him from a dark corner of the lab after I had quietly let myself in on that fateful night. Didn't you think it was strange that the door was locked the next morning? I locked it. I was going to tie up the Professor and then take an axe to his precious Age Altertron. I didn't want any sudden witnesses.

My father sent me, you see. He even paid for the axe.

But guess what? I didn't have to do anything since your friend, the brilliant man of science, did such a good job destroying that machine himself. My father got his wish sort of. But I got a lot more. I could hardly keep myself from laughing as I crawled through the darkness to let myself out through one of the back windows.

But now it doesn't matter. You can know everything. And the most important thing you should know is that your precious gadget will be waiting for you whenever you want to come see me at City Hall. Come there during my office hours and let's do some business together.

Sincerely,
You Know Who

Wayne flicked off the flashlight and stepped out of the closet. "Jackie doesn't want to do business with us, Rodney. He just wants to arrest us."

"You could be right, Wayne. Unless maybe he wants to work out some kind of deal: if we tell him where the Professor is, he'll let us go."

"And then he'll probably make sure that the Age Altertron II gets chopped to pieces. That won't be any kind of a bargain, Rodney."

"You're right. Our freedom in exchange for losing everything and everyone we care about: Aunt Mildred, the Professor. And the next calamity that hits this town just might be our last. And I don't mean that in a good way. Come on. We have to get out of here before Grover and Petey arrive."

Wayne glanced out of the Professor's bedroom window and down at the front gravel drive. The decoys had just ridden up on their bicycles. A car was pulling up behind them. "Uh oh. Too late."

"Not too late. We have at least thirty seconds to get out the back door before whoever is in that car discovers that it isn't you and me on those bikes."

Off the two boys raced through the Professor's large dark house, their eyes better adjusted now to the lack of light.

Meanwhile, in the front yard, bright car lights illuminated Petey and Grover as they started to dismount their bikes. At the same time, three men got out of the car that had been following them. One was Police Chief Rowe. The others were two new police recruits. The two men were very good friends. Only a couple of weeks earlier they had sat next to each other in kindergarten.

"You're not Rodney and Wayne," said Lonnie, looking at Petey and Grover.

"And you have no business being a police chief, you big baboon!" taunted Petey.

"Why Petey!" whispered Grover. "You said the word 'baboon' and some other 'b' words too!"

"I did, didn't I?" said Petey with a proud grin. "Maybe my brain has finally found a way to get around my 'b' problem.

Before Grover could respond, Lonnie barked, "You know what I ought to do? I ought to arrest the both of you!"

"Hey! Lookit! Arrest *them*!" said one of the police chief's officers, pointing at Rodney and Wayne. He had just caught sight of the twins coming through the Professor's backyard gate. The rookie officer was now jumping up and down, both from excitement at spotting the culprits and from having to go to the bathroom.

"We've been tricked!" cried the Police Chief. "Shoot to kill, men."

"Bang! Bang!" said the obedient second officer, pointing the toy gun he had put into his holster in the place of the real one he had been issued.

Lonnie was losing patience. "What is that? Where is your gun?"

He turned to the other officer. "Take your gun, like this…" He cocked the trigger of his own service revolver "And give it to those two criminal house breakers right between the eyes!"

Rodney and Wayne were just rounding the corner of the Professor's backyard fence so they could run off through the adjoining back yard (retracing the route they had taken to get here) when Lonnie Rowe raised his gun and took aim. Part of the beam from the car's headlights shone perfectly upon his two fleeing targets. Grover thought of jumping Lonnie and pinning him to the ground, but there was too much distance between the two of them. Petey had a better, quicker idea. He angled his head so that his steel head plate would catch some of the car's headlight beam and bounce it back into Lonnie's eyes, temporarily blinding the police chief at just the moment that he was about to fire two bullets—one for Rodney and one for Wayne.

"Lookit!" Wayne called to his brother. "Petey's used his own head as a beam deflector!"

Lonnie cursed and tried to block the reflected light with his hand but by then it was too late. Rodney and Wayne had disappeared into the darkness of the adjoining yard.

"Don't just stand there! Go after them!" Lonnie yelled to his two rookies, one of whom was now crying.

"We can't!" said the one who was still dry-eyed.

"Why can't you?"

"Because we're both afraid of the dark!"

"Where are we going?" said Wayne, huffing and puffing at his brother's side.

"To City Hall. I have a feeling that the deflector is somewhere in Jackie's office."

"Why would you think that? Why wouldn't he just toss it away?"

"Because I just thought of another reason that Jackie might want to meet us tomorrow. Something else that he might want to bargain for."

"And what is that, Rodney?"

"Let's stop here, at this picnic table and catch our breaths."

The boys were now in City Park. It was quiet and dark and cool. It was a sweater kind of night. "Don't forget your sweaters, boys!" Rodney could picture his great aunt saying as the two boys rushed out to meet up with their buddies for some moonlight touch football. Sometimes their father would also join them. "And you too, Mitchell!" Aunt Mildred would add. "The night has a nip to it!"

This night had a nip to it too.

"Did you ever think, Wayne, that Jackie might start to get tired of being the mayor of a town in which nobody is younger than fifty-two? And next year will be fifty-three and then fifty-four. We will be an old and dying town for the rest of our days, Wayne. Now at some point, if you were the mayor of a town like that, wouldn't you start to think about maybe turning back the clock a few years— maybe not all the way back, but just far enough back so you'd get to keep your power and your guns and get to keep telling everybody what to do, but still get to be a young man while you're doing it? Remember how much Jackie's father wanted to stay a younger man? So much that he sent Jackie to the Professor's laboratory to destroy the original Age Altertron!"

"I hadn't thought about it, but you're right. It makes sense."

"It actually makes a lot of sense," said a voice from the darkness. The owner of the voice stepped out of the shadows and revealed himself. It was Jackie. "In fact, I was thinking about it this very night."

"What are you doing here?" asked Wayne.

"Well, certainly not chasing after you two. You're a lot faster than I am, I can tell that."

"Lonnie tried to kill us," said Rodney.

"That sounds like Lonnie. He's a juvenile delinquent you know."

"So what are you doing here?" repeated Wayne.

"Sitting here thinking. Remembering how much fun Lonnie and I had turning over all those baby carriages. I miss those days. Simpler times. Good times."

Jackie sat down on the top of the picnic table. He took something out of his pocket and set it down next to him. It was the tertiary beam deflector. "Is this what you guys want?"

Rodney and Wayne nodded, too surprised even to speak.

"And you're right, Rodney. It's a pretty good bargaining chip. So why don't you listen to my proposal and tell me what you think?" Jackie didn't wait for a response. "Give me a year to put things in place—to firm up my hold on this town. One year. And during that year and all the years after that, you two will be free men. You have my promise. Give me that year and then we'll pull the Professor out of mothballs and get him to activate his Age Altertron, and take off, let's say thirty years from all of our ages. I'll be—let's see—thirty-seven then. That's not a bad age to be, don't you think? Think of all the things we could do that our parents would never let us do. And all the things that we could keep *them* from doing for a change."

"There's nothing I can think of that I would want to keep my dad from doing," said Wayne. "I'd be pretty happy just to have him come home!" Wayne stared into a bank of moonlit clouds, his thoughts partly on his father and partly on the tertiary beam deflector he had just slyly picked up and slipped into his pocket.

"And what are you going to give *us*, Jackie?" asked Rodney. "Besides not throwing us in jail for the rest of our lives."

"How about the privilege of working with the Professor, just as you always have, to save this town from future calamities—to be the big heroes two, three times a month. I mean, that's what you guys love, right?"

"I'll tell you what we would love even more," said Rodney. "Not having to live in a town with a Jackie Stovall for a mayor—a town where my Aunt Mildred has to lie on a cot, and nobody knows if they're going to get shot at by your crazy police chief."

"I can't speak for my crazy police chief, monkeys, but I'll tell you this: we'll close that nursing home down the minute we're all young again, and those old folks can start pulling their weight around here again. Scout's honor."

"You were never a Boy Scout, Jackie," said Wayne. "And you know what else, Jackie? I have the deflector in my pocket now. And you know what else? I'm going to knock you right off this picnic table the same way you knocked over all those baby carriages last week." With that, Wayne did exactly what he said he would do. He took a big swing at Jackie that sent him straight to the ground. Then he and Rodney took off.

Out from behind a stand of evergreen trees, several police officers now appeared. "What were you doing back there—playing Tiddly Winks?" Jackie shouted at them and then waved at them to go after Rodney and Wayne. As they ran off, Jackie pulled himself to his feet and massaged his throbbing hip at the place where it had struck the ground. He started walking—with a slight limp—in the direction that Rodney and Wayne and his police officers had gone. He continued his conversation with his twin adversaries as if they

were still there: "I was giving you boys the chance to keep yourselves out of jail! I was giving us all a way to be young again! And
you blew it! You stupid goofball idiot-numskulls!"

Every now and then an officer would fire a shot, but it was too dark
for them to get a good aim, and besides, most of them had never
even picked up a gun before, except a toy cowboy six-shooter. But
Rodney and Wayne weren't taking any chances; they ran faster that
night in their sixty-six-year-old bodies than they had ever run as
thirteen-year-olds.

"*They're* on foot and *we're* on foot," said Wayne panting, as the
boys reached Old Hickory Road.

"So we have to get the upper hand. We have to get a car."

"There's the Professor's house just a block away," said Wayne.

"And lookit! Lonnie's patrol car is gone," said Rodney, noting
the Professor's empty driveway. He grinned. "I'll bet that ol' Nash
will give us just the head start we need to beat Jackie and all of
those nursery school police officers to our house."

Wayne nodded, a big grin curling his own lips.

Rodney raised the garage door. And Wayne drove her out. And she
was beautiful. And Wayne thought it was a shame that there wasn't
time to pull down the top and give the Nash Ambassador convertible the full appreciation she deserved.

Rodney was surprised at what a good driver his brother was.
He only drove up over the curb twice.

The tertiary beam deflector was put into place. And the cover plate was screwed on. And once again the Professor found himself in the frustrating position of having to engage one of his inventions without properly testing it first. But Rodney and Wayne and the Professor had no choice. Jackie and his thugs would soon be at the McCall house. And it would not take long for them to figure it all out—that there had always been a secret room underneath the house—a perfect room for Professor Johnson's new laboratory. And why wouldn't it be? Wasn't the Professor fond of secret cellars? And it would not take Jackie and his men long to find the door and break it down, or they could always remove the floorboards—anything to get to that cellar as quickly as possible and stop the Professor and Rodney and Wayne from activating the new Altertron.

No, there was no time to test the machine, to run the usual diagnostics. And this was a machine that perhaps required even more testing than usual. For the very first time the Professor had delegated the construction of one of his inventions to his two apprentices. Rodney and Wayne McCall, with Professor Johnson's guidance, had put every piece of it together with their own hands. Would the new Age Altertron succeed? There was only one way to find out.

At the City Nursing Home Aunt Mildred lay upon her narrow cot, praying. Former Pitcherville police officer (Loud Noises Unit) Woody Wall, was saying a little prayer himself as he soaked his tired feet in a tub of hot water. At the Ragsdale house Petey and Grover sat Indian-style on the floor of Petey's bedroom surrounded by all the trappings of Petey's boyhood (his model airplanes, his bug collection under glass), their eyes closed tight, their fingers crossed. In the Craft living room Becky waited nervously upon the edge of the sofa, sitting next to her father who was just as nervous as she was. There would be no waiting for midnight this time. Because, as luck would have it, midnight was already there. It came just as the switch was flipped, and within the bat of an eye every Pitchervillian was returned to the age he was before.

Aunt Mildred sat straight up on her cot and let out a happy yell. Others around her sat up as well, and when they realized what had happened, they started to hoot and yip and jump up and down in their now much younger bodies. Officer Wall felt the pain lift from his soaking feet. Becky touched her neck to find it smooth and youthful again. Petey and Grover felt the tops of their heads and discovered hair—and two quite bushy mops of hair at that!

And standing next to the machine that Rodney and Wayne had built, the machine that finally saved the town of Pitcherville from its worst calamity yet, Rodney looked into the face of his brother and saw his mirror image, and Wayne looked at Rodney in the same way, and each twin was pleased to see a reflection in the other of his own boyish grin.

As for Jackie Stovall and Lonnie Rowe—well, we'll tell what became of them in the very next book.

RODNEY'S NOTEBOOK

What we learned from the Age Changer-Deranger-Estranger:

1.) The calamities are getting harder to correct. Being eighteen months old one day then being sixty-six the very next day is much harder than being the color of peaches.

2.) The calamities are getting more dangerous. Several old people almost died and I bruised both of my knees learning how to walk all over again.

3.) The Unknown Entity took our Dad but it also took his diorama "Democracity II," even though it wasn't finished yet. Why did they want to see it? Is he still working on it?

4.) Why can't I call my Grandpa and Grandma McCall on the phone but Aunt Mildred gets to listen to her radio shows and Petey gets to watch his wrestling shows on TV and Wayne and I get to keep watching our cowboy shows?

5.) Petey and the other young children were taken to a special place without walls or floors. A place where they floated as if they were in space, where there was nothing but a telephone. Where is this place?

6.) Are Jackie and Lonnie working for the Unknown Entity? Lonnie is too stupid. But maybe Jackie...

The End

ACKNOWLEDGMENTS

The author wishes to thank the following individuals for helping to launch this new book series through their support and valuable input: my wife Mary; Ariel, Jake, and Laura Atlas; Kira and Pat Gabridge; and Jack Walsh. The author also wishes to thank his literary agent Amy Rennert and his editor David Adams, as well as his publisher David Poindexter and editor-in-chief at MacAdam/Cage Pat Walsh, for their many years of dedicated support to this quixotic scribbler.